Rose never imagined her entire life would change in a heartbeat.

Near midnight, Mommy fell asleep beside me. My heart did flip-flops when I saw the car headlights pulling into our driveway. *Daddy,* I thought. *Finally.*

But when I stepped up to the window, I saw it wasn't Daddy. It was a police car with the emblem on the side identifying it as a Georgia State Police vehicle. Two officers stepped out, put on their hats, and walked toward our front door. For a moment, I couldn't move; I couldn't breathe.

The sound of the door buzzer made Mommy's eyelids flutter.

"Was that our front door?"

"Yes, Mommy," I said. I couldn't swallow.

"Well, who would be here at this hour?"

I glanced out the window and then back at her....

ROSE

V.C. Andrews® Books

The Dollanganger Family Series
Flowers in the Attic
Petals on the Wind
If There Be Thorns
Seeds of Yesterday
Garden of Shadows

The Casteel Family Series
Heaven
Dark Angel
Fallen Hearts
Gates of Paradise
Web of Dreams

The Cutler Family Series
Dawn
Secrets of the Morning
Twilight's Child
Midnight Whispers
Darkest Hour

The Landry Family Series
Ruby
Pearl in the Mist
All That Glitters
Hidden Jewel
Tarnished Gold

The Logan Family Series
Melody
Heart Song
Unfinished Symphony
Music in the Night
Olivia

The Orphans Miniseries
Butterfly
Crystal
Brooke
Raven
Runaways (full-length novel)

The Wildflowers Miniseries
Misty
Star
Jade
Cat
Into the Garden (full-length novel)

The Hudson Family Series
Rain
Lightning Strikes
Eye of the Storm
The End of the Rainbow

The Shooting Stars Series
Cinnamon
Ice
Rose

My Sweet Audrina
(does not belong to a series)

Published by POCKET BOOKS

POCKET BOOKS
New York London Toronto Sydney Singapore

For information regarding special discounts for bulk purchases, please contact Simon & Schuster Special Sales at 1-800-456-6798 or business@simonandschuster.com

Following the death of Virginia Andrews, the Andrews family worked with a carefully selected writer to organize and complete Virginia Andrews' stories and to create additional novels, of which this is one, inspired by her storytelling genius.

This book is a work of fiction. Names, characters, places and incidents are products of the author's imagination or are used fictitiously. Any resemblance to actual events or locales or persons, living or dead, is entirely coincidental.

An *Original* Publication of POCKET BOOKS

POCKET BOOKS, a division of Simon & Schuster, Inc.
1230 Avenue of the Americas, New York, NY 10020

ISBN: 0-671-03995-4

First Pocket Books paperback printing September 2001

10 9 8 7 6 5 4 3 2 1

Front cover illustration by Lisa Falkenstern

Printed in the U.S.A.

Rose

Prologue

When I was a little girl, I thought the bogeyman was hiding in shadows, watching for an opportunity to scare or hurt me. He lived in the darkness. I saw him in the quick movement of a silhouette, heard him tiptoeing over creaky floorboards or whispering through the walls. He entered my mind through nightmares and made me whimper and cry out for my mother or my father.

When I grew older and wiser, I realized the bogeyman is not in the shadows, not in the darkness outside. He is in the hearts of evil people, selfish and envious people, and they urge him to frighten or hurt us. They whisper our names into his ear and point him in our direction.

And the only weapon we have against him is the power of love. We can turn it on him like a great light and chase him back into the evil hearts that gave him life.

It was a lesson I learned painfully. It took away my innocence and my trusting heart. It made me cautious and skeptical. I questioned every smile, every laugh, every kind word, scrutinizing all to be sure the bogeyman wasn't somehow involved.

I had to become older, mature, and be strong.

But how I longed for my childhood faith and the simple wonder that came with the sun that woke me to every new day.

It was hard to leave all that behind.

It was the saddest good-bye of all.

1

Daddy

I always believed there was something different about my father. He was whimsical and airy, light of foot and so smooth and graceful, he could slip in and out of a room full of people without anyone realizing he was gone. I don't think I ever saw him depressed or even deeply concerned about anything, no matter how dark the possibilities were. He lost jobs, had cars repossessed, saw his homes go into foreclosure. Twice, that I knew of, he was forced to declare personal bankruptcy. There was even a time when we left one of our homes with little more than we carried on our very selves. Yet he never lost his spirit or betrayed his unhappiness in his voice.

I used to imagine him as a little boy stumbling and rolling over and over until he stopped and jumped right to his feet, smiling, with his arms out and singing a big "Ta-da!" as if his accident was an accomplishment. He was actually expecting applause, laughter, and encouragement after a fiasco. He once told me that when he received a failing grade on a test in school, he took joy in having a bright red mark on his paper while the other, less fortunate students who happened to have passed had only the common black. Defeat was never in his vocabulary. Every mistake, every failure was merely a minor setback, and what was a setback anyway? Just an opportunity to start anew. Pity the poor successful ones who spent their whole lives in one town, in one job, in one house.

Daddy, I would learn, carried that idea even into the concept of family.

He was a handsome man in a Harrison Ford sort of way, not perfect, but surprising because his pastel blue eyes could suddenly brighten with a burst of happy energy that made his smile magnetic, his laughter musical, and his every gesture as graceful as a bull fighter's. He stood six feet one, with an unruly shock of flaxen-blond hair that somehow never looked messy, but instead always looked interesting, making someone think that here was a man who had just run a mile or fought a great fight. He was athletic-looking, trim with firm shoulders. He never had the patience or the discipline to be a good school athlete when he was young, but he was not above stopping whatever he was doing, no matter how important, and joining some teenagers in the neighborhood to play a game of driveway basketball.

Daddy's impulsiveness and childlike joy in leaping out of one persona into another in an instant annoyed my mother to no end. She always seemed embarrassed by his antics and depressed by his failures, yet she held onto him like someone clinging to a wayward sailboat in a storm, hoping the wind would die down, the rain would stop, and soon, maybe just over the horizon, there would be sunny skies. On what she built these sails full of optimism, I never knew. Maybe that was her fantasy: believing in Daddy, a fantasy I thought belonged only to a young and innocent daughter, me.

Or maybe it was just impossible to be anything but optimistic around Daddy. I truly never saw him sulk and rarely saw him look disgusted. Of course, I never saw him cry. He wasn't even angry at the people who fired him from his jobs or the events that turned him out of one opportunity after another. It was always a big "Oh, well, let's just move on."

At least we remained in one state, Georgia, crisscrossing and vaulting towns, cities, villages; however, it soon became obvious that Daddy anticipated his inevitable defeats. After a while—our second mortgage failure, I think—we stopped buying and started renting for as short a period as the landlords tolerated. Daddy loved six-month leases. He called every new rental a trial period, a romance. Who knew if it was what we wanted or if it would last, so why get too committed? Why get committed to anything?

Of course, Mommy flung the usual arguments at him.

"Rose needs a substantial foundation. She can't do well in school, moving like this from place to place. She can't make friends, and neither can I, Charles.

"And neither can you!" she emphasized, her eyebrows nearly leaping off her face. "You don't do anything with other men like most men do. You don't watch ball games or go out hunting and fishing with buddies and it's no wonder. You don't give yourself a chance to build a friendship, a relationship. Before you see someone for the second time, you're packing suitcases."

My father would listen as if he was really giving all that serious thought and then he would shake his head and say something like, "There's no such thing as friends anyway, just acquaintances, Monica."

"Good. Let me at least have a long enough life somewhere to have acquaintances," Mommy fired back at him.

He laughed and nodded.

"You will," he promised. "You will."

Daddy made promises like children blow bubbles. At the first suggestion of approaching storm clouds, he blew his promises at us, perfectly shaped, rainbow-colored hopes and dreams, and stood back watching them float and bob around us. When they popped, he just reached into his bag of tricks and started a new bubble. I felt like we were all swimming in a glass of champagne.

Bursting through the front door at the end of his workday, whatever it happened to be, he cried out his wonderful "I'm home!" He bellowed like someone who expected everything would be dropped. Mommy and I would come running out of rooms with music blaring behind us. She would put down her magazine or book, or stop working on dinner. I would leap from my desk where I was doing homework or spring from the sofa where I was sprawled watching television, and we would rush into the hallway to hug him and be hugged by him.

That stopped happening so long ago, I couldn't remember if we had ever done it. Now when he bellowed his "I'm home," his voice echoed and died. He still greeted us with his big, happy smile, looking like someone who had returned from the great wars when all he had done was finish one more day of new work successfully enough not to get laid off.

At present, he was a car salesman in Lewisville, Georgia, a small community about forty-five miles northwest of Atlanta famous for its duck ponds and its one industry, Lewis Foundry, which manufactures automotive cast-iron braking components and employs over seven hundred people. Small housing developments sprouted up around it and from that blossomed retail shops, a mall, and four automobile distributorships, one for which, Kruegar's, Daddy worked selling vans and suburban vehicles and Jeeps.

How Daddy found these places was always a mystery to us, but for the past two years, which was a record, we had been living here in a small house we rented. It was actually the most comfortable and largest home we had ever owned or rented. It was a Queen Anne with a gabled roof and a front porch. It had a small backyard, an attached garage, a half-basement, and an attic. There were three bedrooms, a nice size dining room, a kitchen with appliances that still functioned, and a modest living room. Since we didn't have all that much furniture anyway, it was quite adequate for our needs, and the street was quiet, the neighbors pleasant and friendly.

Everyone liked Daddy pretty much instantly. He was so outgoing and amiable, always greeting them with a smile and a hello full of interest. Daddy was a glib man. He could stop and talk politics, economics, books and movies, and especially hunting and fishing with anyone. He always knew just enough to sound educated on an issue, but not really enough for any deep analysis. He hadn't gone to college, but he knew how to agree with people, to anticipate what they felt and thought, and find ways to escort them down their paths of beliefs, making them think he was a sympathetic voice, in sync with whatever theory or analysis they had. Mommy always said Daddy missed his calling. He should have been a politician. He even could talk his way out of a speeding ticket. By the time he was finished, the poor policeman almost felt guilty.

Daddy's verbal skills and friendly manner did make him a good salesman. When he failed at a sales job, it wasn't because he couldn't do it. I always thought it was either because he lost interest or saw something over the horizon that attracted him more. He would slack off and eventually cause his boss to decide it would be better if Daddy moved on, and move on he did. Daddy was so agreeable, I'm sure his bosses found firing him was almost a cheerful experience.

Now, we were here, still here, hoping to stay, hoping to build a life. Mommy was permitting herself to make close friends, to join organizations, to make commitments. I was doing well in school, and since I was at the beginning of my senior year, we were expecting I would graduate at this high school. I hadn't yet decided what I wanted to do with my life. I had been in school plays and I was told I had an impressive stage presence and carried myself like a seasoned fashion model, but I knew I didn't have a strong enough voice, and I was never very comfortable memorizing lines and pretending to be someone else.

Mommy didn't pressure me to be anything special. Her advice was more along the lines of what to do with myself socially. Lately, she was more strident-sounding than ever with her warnings.

"Don't give your heart to anyone until the last moment, and then think it over three times."

Her dark pronouncements came from her own regret in having married so young and ending what she called her chance for really living before she had even started. She and Daddy had been high school sweethearts and consequently married soon after graduation, despite the admonishments of her parents, who refused to pay for any wedding. Daddy and she eloped and set up house as soon as he acquired the first of what was to be a long string of jobs.

Because of our lifestyle, I knew that Mommy now considered herself well beyond her prime. I could see it in her eyes whenever she and I went anywhere. She would take furtive glances at men to see if they were looking her way, following her movements with their eyes, showing any interest. If a younger woman pulled their attention from her, the disappointment would settle in her face like a rock in mud, and she would want to get our shopping over quickly and go home to brood.

Over the years, she had taken odd jobs working in department stores, especially in the cosmetic departments, because she was a very attractive woman. When Daddy lost his positions, Mommy would have to give up hers, no matter how well she was doing or how pleased her bosses were with her work. After this happened a number of times, Mommy simply gave up trying to work.

"What is the point?" she asked Daddy. "I won't be able to hold down the job or get promoted."

"I'd rather have you at home anyway, my homemaker, Rose's full-time mother," Daddy declared, avoiding any argument. He acted as if the added income was superfluous, when it sometimes was all we had.

Now, because we had lived in Lewisville so long, Mommy was considering returning to work. I was old enough to take care of my own needs, to help out in the house, and she had lots of free time to fill. Daddy didn't oppose her when she brought all this up now. In fact, they rarely had marital spats. Daddy was too easy for that. He would never disagree vehemently. Nothing seemed to matter that much to him, nothing deserved his raising his voice, putting on an angry face, sulking or being in the slightest way unhappy. His reaction to it all was always a shrug and a simple, "Whatever."

It had become our family motto. Whatever I wanted; whatever Mommy wanted. Whatever the world wanted of us, it was fine with Daddy. He loved that old adage, "If a branch doesn't bend, it breaks."

"How about not breaking, Charles, but not having to bend either?" Mommy asked him.

He shook his head, smiling.

"Monica, there's no place in the world where there's never a wind."

Mommy showed her frustration and started to go into a depression and brood, but Daddy would come up with that rabbit in his hat almost all the time. He would have flowers sent to her, or he would secretly buy her some new perfume or some piece of jewelry. She would shake her head and call him an idiot, but she was always too pleased to keep up her growling. In the end, Daddy's charm overwhelmed everything. I started to believe he might be right about life. There was nothing worth stress. He lived the Edith Piaf song he played when he sat quietly with his martini in the living room. *Je Regret Rien:* I regret nothing.

Whatever happened, happened. It was over and done with, in the past. Forget it. Look to the future. It was a philosophy of life that turned every rainy day into a sunny one. You put your Band-Aids on your scrapes and bruises, choked back tears, and forgot about them.

"There should be only happy tears, anyway," Daddy told me once. "What does crying get you? If you're miserable, you're defeating yourself. Laugh at life and you'll always be on top of things, Rose."

I looked at him with wonder, my Daddy, the magician who seemed incapable of *not* finding rainbows. The ease with which he captured people impressed me, but what impressed me more was the ease with which he tossed it all away or gave it up once he had succeeded. Was that ability to let go with no regret a power or a madness? I wondered. Was nothing worth holding onto at any cost? Was nothing worth tears?

It wasn't long before I had an answer.

According to Mommy, it was Daddy who insisted on naming me Rose, quoting one of his favorite Shakespearean lines, "A rose by any other name would smell as sweet." It wasn't only because he insisted I had the sweetest face of any baby born that day. He argued that a rose always brought happiness, good times, bright and wonderful things.

"What happens whenever you place a rose next to something?" he asked her in the hospital. "Huh? I'll tell you, Monica. It makes it seem more wonderful, more delicious, more enticing, and more desirable. That's what will happen every time she comes into a room or into anyone's life. That's our Rose."

Mommy said she gave in because she had never seen him so excited and determined about anything as much as he was about my name. She said my grandparents thought it was just dreadful to have a name like that on a birth certificate.

"She's a little girl, not a flower," Grandfather Wallace, Daddy's father, had declared. He favored old names, names garnered from ancestors, but Daddy had long since lost the ties with family that most people enjoy. His father never approved of the things he did with his life. Both of his parents closed all the blinds on every window that looked out on him. They shut down like a clam, but Daddy didn't mourn the loss.

"People who drag you down, who are negative people, are dangerous," Daddy told me when I asked him about my grandparents and why we had so little to do with them. "Who needs that? Before long, they make you sad sacks, too. No sad sacks for us!" he cried and swung me around.

When I was a little girl, he was always hugging me or twirling my strawberry blond hair in his fingers, telling me that I was a jewel.

"Your eyes are two diamonds. Your hair is spun gold. Your lips are rubies and your skin comes from pearls. My Rose petal," he cried and kissed the tip of my nose. Laughter swirled in his eyes and dazzled me. Everything my daddy did was fascinating to me in those early years. He even made every meal we had a special event, assigning names and stories to each and every thing we ate. Mommy told him I laughed too much at dinner and I would have stomachaches, but Daddy didn't believe that happy things could do any harm in any way.

"Glum people have stomachaches, Monica. We don't, right, Rose?" he would ask.

Of course, I always agreed with him then. To me it seemed the right thing to do, the right way to go, the right way to be: carefree, happy, unconcerned.

"Your father just never grew up," my mother told me. "He's a little boy in a man's body. Yes, he makes people feel good, but one of these days, he's going to have to become substantial. I just hope it's soon," she would tell me.

Worry darkened her eyes. She took her deep breaths and waited, worked when she could, and made the best of every home we had, but I couldn't help feeling this same anxiety as I grew older and wiser and saw the shine begin to dull on Daddy's face and ways. Despite his attitudes and behavior, he was growing older. Gray hairs sounded small warnings and began to sprout like weeds in that flaxen cornfield. Lines were deepening under his eyes. He was less and less apt to drop everything and rush onto a basketball court to match himself against young boys. The world he had kept at bay was seeping in and under every door. He was beginning to show wear and tear. He had to search harder and harder to find ways to deny it, or avoid it.

Daddy kept his little escapes private. He did a little more drinking than Mommy liked, but he didn't do it in salons and dingy bars with degenerate friends. He kept his whiskey in a paper bag and drank surreptitiously. Even his drinking was solitary. All of his means of relaxation were. He loved to go duck hunting, but he never went with a group. He was a true loner when it came to all this. It was as if he didn't want to share those moments of doubt or admit that he needed his retreats from reality.

One weekend morning, as usual, he rose early and left the house before Mommy and I rose. He didn't leave a note or any indication about where he had gone, but it was fall and duck season, so we knew he was off to some solitary place he had discovered, some little outlet from which he could launch his rowboat and sit waiting for the ducks. He never shot more than we could eat, and Mommy was very good at preparing duck. She said it made him feel like some great hunter providing for his family. He was always saying that if we had to return to the days of the pioneers, he was equipped to do so.

The night before he went hunting, he had come into my room while I was doing my homework. I had started it on a Friday night because I had been given a lot to do over the weekend, including beginng a social studies term paper. He stood there a while, watching me quietly, before I realized he had entered. He smiled at my surprise.

"Daddy? What?" I asked him.

He shook his head and sat beside me on the floor with his legs curled up under him. It had been a while since he had done this. Unlike the parents of most of my friends, Daddy didn't hover over me daily or even on a weekly basis checking on my schoolwork and questioning my social activities. In some of the houses of my school friends, their parents behaved like FBI agents. One girl revealed that her parents had actually bugged her telephone because they suspected she was in with a bad crowd, and another told me her parents had hired a private detective who followed her when she went out on dates. She said it was by pure accident that she had discovered it. She inadvertently pressed the answering machine playback in her father's office and heard the detective's report about her most recent date.

These parents made me feel grateful I had a father who was so casual and trusting. Nothing I did ever displeased him greatly. He didn't yell. He never even so much as threatened to hit me, and if my mother imposed a punishment like "Go to your room for the night," or "Stay in all weekend," my father would intercede to say, "She knows she's made a mistake, Monica. What's the point?"

Frustrated, my mother would throw up her hands and tell him to take charge and be responsible. Daddy would turn his big, soft eyes on me and say, "Don't get me in trouble, Rose. Please, behave." I think that plea of his, more than anything, kept me from misbehaving. It was funny how I hated the idea of Daddy ever being sad. If he should be, it would seem as if the world had come crashing down on us. I was afraid that once my daddy lost his smile, the sunshine would be gone from our lives.

"There's nothing in particular," Daddy replied to my question when he sat on the floor beside me. "But it's Friday night. How come you're not going anywhere with your friends—a movie, a dance? You're probably the most beautiful girl in the school."

"I'm going out with Paula Conrad tomorrow night, Daddy, remember? I told you and Mommy at dinner."

"Oh. Right."

He smiled.

"Just you and Paula?"

"We'll probably go to a movie and meet some other kids."

He nodded.

"And I assume other kids includes boys."

"Yes, Daddy."

"So how are you really doing these days, Rose? Are you happy here?"

A small patter of alarm began in my heart. Daddy often began a conversation this way when he was going to explain why we were about to move.

"Everything is good, Daddy. I like my teachers and I'm doing well in my classes. You saw my first report card this year, all A's. I've never gotten all A's before, Daddy," I pointed out.

He nodded, pressing his lips tightly.

"And I was in the school plays last year, so I was thinking of going out for the big musical in the spring. The drama teacher keeps reminding me. I don't know why. I can't sing that well."

"You're the jewel, Rose. He wants his show to sparkle," Daddy said, smiling. "Don't be too humble," he warned. "Act like sheep and they'll act like wolves," he warned.

I knew he was right, but I was afraid to wish anything big for myself. I guess I've always been modest and shy. Maybe that was because I was afraid of committing myself to anything that required a long-term effort. We had been so nomadic, moving like gypsies from town to town, city to city, so often I was terrified of becoming too close to anyone or too involved in any activity. Good-byes were like tiny pins jabbed into my heart. How many times had I sat in the rear of the car looking through the back window at the home I had just known as it disappeared around a bend and was gone forever?

However, Daddy wasn't the only one who used superlatives when remarking about my looks. I should have been building up my confidence. Wherever Mommy took me, even when I was only six or seven, people complimented me on my features, my complexion, my eyes. I was often told how photogenic I was, and how I should be on the covers of magazines.

When I was about eleven, I sensed that my male teachers looked at me and spoke to me differently from the way they did the other students and especially the other girls. I could feel the pleasure I brought merely being in front of them. In my early teen years, my male teachers seemed to flirt with me. Other girls with green eyes of envy muttered about my being Mr. Potter's pet or Mr. Conklin's special girl. They complained that I could do no wrong in the opinion of my male teachers. They even assumed my grades were inflated because I knew how to bat my long, perfect eyelashes or smile softly so that my eyes were sexy, inviting.

I suppose it was inevitable that Mommy would want to enter me in a beauty contest. Six months after we had arrived in Lewisville, Mommy heard about the Miss Lewisville Foundry beauty pageant and discovered that through some oversight there was no minimum age requirement. She decided I could compete with women in their late teens and twenties and filled out the application. She made Daddy ask his boss to consider sponsoring me, and I was brought to the dealership to meet Mr. Kruegar, a balding forty-year-old man who had inherited the business from his father. It was the first time I was paraded in front of someone who looked at me like some commodity, a product—in his case, like a brand-new car. He even referred to me as he would refer to one of his new model vehicles.

"She has the chassis. That's for sure, Charles," he said, drinking me in from head to foot, pausing over my breasts and my waist as if he was measuring me for a dress. "Nice bumpers and great chrome," he added and quickly laughed. "You're a beautiful girl, Rose. No wonder your father's proud of you. Sure we'll sponsor her, Charles. She's a winner and I can't get hurt by the publicity. Not if she's going to wear a Kruegar T-shirt and a Kruegar pin. That's for sure."

Mr. Kruegar wiped the tip of his tongue over his

thick, wet lips and nodded as he continued to scrutinize me with his beady eyes. I felt like a dinner for a cannibal and wanted nothing more to do with the contest or him, but Mommy assured me he would have little to do with what happened.

"You probably won't see him again until the actual event," she promised.

With a good budget now for my preparations, Mommy set out to buy me an attractive evening dress, a new bathing suit, and a pretty blouse and skirt outfit. The contest took only one day. Like the Miss America pageant, there was the question and answer period, which at least pretended an interest in our minds as well as our bodies. Then there was the swimsuit competition, and finally, the evening when we could sing, read poems, dance, whatever. I did a Hawaiian folk dance I learned off a videotape Mommy had bought. After we were all finished with our talent show, we paraded in front of the judges for the final evaluation, supposedly based upon poise and grace.

I knew the older women were infuriated that I had been entered. None of them were friendly. As it turned out, a woman named Sheila Stowe won the title. I was first runner-up. Everyone in the audience, except Sheila's family, thought I was cheated because Sheila, as it turned out, was a relative of the Lewis family.

After the contest, people insisted on calling me Ms. Lewisville Foundry or just Miss Foundry whenever they saw me. They sympathized with my mother, cajoling and insisting I was the true beauty of Lewisville. I can't say it didn't put daydreams in my head. I began to imagine myself on the covers of the biggest and most glamorous magazines, eventually developing products under my name. I started to think of elegance and style more seriously, and began to dare ambition.

"I'm expecting you to become someone very special, Rose," Daddy told me as he sat there in my room. "I have high hopes. I know that I haven't exactly made things easy for you and your mother, but," he said, smiling, "you're like some powerful, magnificent flower plowing itself up between the rocks, finding the sunshine and blooming with blossoms richer than those of flowers in perfectly prepared gardens. Just believe in yourself," he advised.

Daddy hardly ever spoke so seriously to me. It kept my heart thumping.

"I'll try, Daddy," I said.

"Sure you will. Sure," he said. He played with the loose ends of my bedroom floor rug for a moment, holding his soft, gentle smile. "I guess I never had much faith in myself. I guess I move on so much because I'm afraid of making too much of an investment in anything. It would make failure look like failure," he said, looking up, "instead of just a temporary setback I can ignore.

"Don't be like me, Rose. Dig your heels into something and stick with it, okay?"

"Okay, Daddy," I said.

He stood up, leaned over, and kissed me on the forehead, twirling my hair in his forefinger and reciting: "Your eyes are two diamonds. Your hair is spun gold. Your lips are rubies and your skin comes from pearls. My Rose petal."

He laughed, kissed me again, and walked out.

I never heard his voice again or his laugh or bathed in his happy smile.

2

Gone

Mommy was up almost as early as Daddy Saturday morning. When I came down to breakfast, she told me she must have just missed him. She was sitting at the table, flipping the pages of her cookbook, searching for a new and interesting recipe for duck.

"I'm tired of having duck, but if we don't eat what he brings home, he'll make me feel like I've committed a sin, having him kill a duck for nothing."

"You always make it delicious, Mommy," I said.

"Um," she replied, her eyes on the recipe she had found. "I've got to go to the supermarket to get some of these ingredients."

"I'm going to the movies tonight with Paula Conrad," I reminded her.

She nodded, half-listening.

"Mommy. Daddy didn't say anything about us having to move soon, did he?" I asked, and she brought her head up so fast, I thought she would snap her neck.

"No, why?"

"I don't know. He was talking so..."

"What?"

"Seriously. I just got that feeling," I said.

"I won't go. I won't," she insisted. "This time, I'm going to plant my feet in cement. I've got an interview with Mr. Weinberg who owns that insurance agency on Grant Street. He's looking for a receptionist and bookkeeper and I can make a good salary. I won't go.

"Besides," she continued, "you've got to finish your senior year here. Did he actually suggest moving?"

I shook my head.

"It was just a feeling I got, Mommy."

"Um," she said, her eyes narrowing with suspicion. "I should be wary. Whenever he starts going off by himself regularly on weekends and increases his drinking, it usually means something. No one can blame me for being paranoid," she added.

She sat there, pensive for a long quiet moment, and then she slammed her palm down on the table so hard, she made the dishes jump and clang.

"I'm not going and that's final."

She rose and marched out of the kitchen before I could even try to calm her down. I felt guilty for putting her ill at ease and probably clawing and barking at Daddy the moment he returned from hunting. All day long she built up her fury. I could see it in the brightening fire in her eyes and could hear it in the way she pounded through the house, slammed doors, and ran the vacuum cleaner. She was pressing down so hard on the handle, I was sure she was sucking up the very foundation of the house.

Early in the afternoon, she set out for the supermarket. She asked me to go along. I was afraid even to hesitate. It was an unusually warm day for late October, with just a few puffs of cotton white clouds barely moving across the turquoise sky. The world looked so vibrant, all the colors sharp and rich in the grass, the flowers, the picket fences. Days like this encouraged people to wash their cars, cut their lawns, paint and spruce up their homes. The freshness and the sharpness around us underscored how good we both felt about our present home and how much we wanted to hold on to it.

"How could he even dare to contemplate a move now?" Mommy muttered.

Once again, I emphasized that I didn't know he was for sure. It was just a feeling.

She looked at me and nodded, convinced of the worst possible scenario.

"He is," she said. "You're right on it. I live in denial most of the time and ignore all the signals until they're plopped right in my face.

"I'll make him a duck dinner," she fumed, making it sound more like a threat. "I'll make him a duck dinner he'll never forget."

She carried her fury into the supermarket and stomped around the aisles, pushing the cart like a lawn mower, plowing anyone in her way to the right or to the left before they had to meet her head-on. When anyone said hello, she fired her hello back as if they had cursed her. Her reply of "I'm fine, thank you very much," was almost a challenge to declare otherwise. I saw some people shake their heads as we continued by.

At the checkout counter, Jimmy Slater gave me his usual big grin as he packed my mother's groceries.

"How's Miss Lewisville Foundry today?" he asked me.

"I'm not Miss Lewisville Foundry," I said for the hundredth time.

"You are to me," Jimmy insisted.

My mother glanced at him with her eyes askance and almost smiled at me as we headed out to the car. At home I helped her unpack and put away our groceries, and then I went up to my room to continue my homework. Around five o'clock, I expected to hear Daddy's Jeep pulling into the driveway with its usual squeal of tires. I leaned toward my window, which faced the front of our house, and looked down, anticipating his arrival any moment. At five-fifteen, I heard Mommy pacing in the downstairs hallway.

"If that man expects a duck dinner tonight, he'd better be here in five minutes," she declared. "I don't serve greasy duck. It takes a few hours to make it right."

She pounded back to the kitchen and then, twenty minutes later, she returned to the living room to look out the front windows. I came down the stairway and stood in the living room doorway. She was standing there, her arms folded, glaring at the street. For a long moment, neither of us moved or spoke. Then she turned and looked at me, her face twisted with anxiety and anger.

"I don't know why I'm surprised. Why should time matter to a man like that now? It never has before," she said.

I glanced at the miniature grandfather clock on the mantel above our small fireplace. It was now five-forty-five. Twilight deepened. Shadows were spreading like broken egg yolks over the street.

"You go make yourself something to eat. I know you're going to the movies," Mommy told me.

I nodded and went to the kitchen, but I had very little appetite. My anxiety over what would go on when Daddy returned had turned my stomach into a ball of knotted string. Every once in a while my heart would pitter-patter like a downpour of rain against a window.

Six o'clock came and went and still we were waiting for Daddy's Jeep to pull in. Mommy came into the kitchen and banged some pots and pans and then started to put things away.

"If he thinks I'm going to make a duck dinner now, he's got another think coming," she muttered.

At six-thirty, Mommy's lines of anger began to slip and slide off her face to be replaced by folds of anxiety and concern in her forehead. Small flashes of panic lit her eyes as she walked back to the front windows.

"Where is he?" she cried.

When the phone rang, we both looked at it for a moment. Then I lifted the receiver. It was Paula, telling me she would be by to pick me up at ten after seven. I looked at Mommy. I couldn't leave her until Daddy had arrived, I thought.

"I can't go, Paula."

"What? Why not? We're supposed to be meeting Ed Wiley and Barry Burton. We practically promised, Rose."

"I can't go. My father hasn't gotten home yet from hunting ducks and we're worried about him," I said.

She was silent.

"Oh, go to the movies," Mommy said. "You're not going to do me any good sitting here and clutching your hands. I'll eat something and watch television. I'm sure he's just gone a little farther this time."

"Why wouldn't he call us, Mommy?"

"Why? Why? Don't start asking me why your father does this or that. We'll be here forever thinking of answers. Go on. Be with your friends."

"Are you sure?"

"Yes," she insisted.

"Okay, Paula," I said. "Come on over to get me."

"Good," Paula said and hung up before I could change my mind.

I didn't see how I was going to have a good time, but I went up to fix my hair and put on some makeup. At seven o'clock, Mommy hovered over a plate of cold salmon and some salad, but she had eaten very little.

"Two hours late, Mommy."

"I can read a clock, Rose. When he comes through that door, I'm going to hit him over the head with it, in fact," she threatened. I knew it was a very empty threat. When he came through that door, all the air she was holding in her lungs would be released and all the tension in her body would fly out. We both spun as if we were on springs when we heard a car pull into the driveway.

"See if that's him," she ordered, and I went out to look. It was only Paula arriving a little early.

Paula was tall and slim with long dark brown hair and round hazel eyes. She was the captain of the girls' basketball team and very popular in school. The real reason we were going out together was that the boy she was after, Ed Wiley, was best friends with Barry Burton, who I heard was interested in me, but was very shy. Paula had practically begged me to go out with her.

"Hi," she cried enthusiastically as soon as I opened the door.

My mother stood in the hallway, her arms folded, gazing at us and forcing a smile onto her face. Paula looked from her to me and raised her eyebrows.

"Your father still not back?"

I shook my head.

"He'll be fine. Don't worry about it," Mommy assured me. "Go on. Have a good time, girls."

"Thank you, Mrs. Wallace," Paula replied instantly.

Was her budding romance so important to her that she could ignore our worries? I wondered. One look at her told me most definitely.

"Let's go," she urged, practically pulling me out the door.

I glanced back at Mommy and felt so terrible leaving her.

"Go on," she ordered in a loud whisper.

"I'll call after the movies, Mommy," I promised. She nodded and we left.

Paula babbled about the boys all the way to the theater complex. I was only half-listening. Daddy's behavior the night before had made me nervous, and his considerable lateness on top of that had practically turned me inside out.

"Stop worrying," Paula finally cried as we drew closer to the movies. "He's probably with some of his buddies in some bar. My father's done that dozens of times."

"My father hasn't," I said dryly.

She shook her head and looked at me as if I lived in a bubble.

When we arrived at the theater, the boys were waiting in the lobby. Paula went right after Ed, swooping in on him as if she was afraid to let him have a moment without her voice in his ear and her face in his eyes. He looked overwhelmed, and glanced back at Barry, who just smiled and escorted me quietly to our seats. I liked Barry well enough. He was a good-looking boy and seemed very nice. His shyness was actually calming and refreshing. Most of the boys I knew thought they were God's gift to women and spent more time on their coiffure, complexion, and clothes than most of the girls.

But I was a poor date this night. Even the movie,

an exciting thriller about a woman and her seven-year-old daughter imprisoned by a mad family after her car broke down on an old country road, didn't keep my attention. My mind continually drifted back to Mommy standing in that hallway, looking so small and fragile under the cloak of fear and anxiety. I couldn't wait for the show to end so I could get to the pay phone to call her.

She answered on the first ring, which told me she was hovering over the phone in anticipation.

"Mommy, isn't he back?"

"No," she said, her voice cracking. "I don't know what to do. Should I call the police? I just know what they'll do about it...nothing, I bet. A man doesn't come home to his wife for hours. That's probably not so uncommon, but your father hasn't done something like this before. He's done lots of things I could wring his neck over, but this isn't something he's done. Of course, there's no telling if he's starting some new outrage for me to tolerate."

I realized she was babbling to me.

"Call the police anyway, Mommy," I said. "Let them be the ones to tell you not to worry, but at least let them be aware of your concern."

"I don't know. It's embarrassing," she said. "But maybe you're right. Maybe..."

"Do it, Mommy," I insisted.

Finally, she agreed and hung up.

I turned to the others.

"I've got to go home," I said.

"What?" Paula cried, her face practically sliding off her skull. "We're going to get some pizza and then we're going to Ed's house and..."

"I've got to go home," I repeated. "I'm sorry. My father hasn't come home from hunting and it's almost ten o'clock. My mother's calling the police."

"Wow!" Ed said.

"Oh pooh," Paula groaned.

"I'll take her home. You two go for pizza," Barry said.

"Really? Okay," Paula said quickly. She scooped her arm into Ed's. "We'll just go ahead in my car." She practically tugged him out of the movie lobby.

"Thanks," I told Barry.

We left the theater quickly.

"I'm sorry to spoil everyone's good time," I said after we got into his car.

"No problem. There'll be other good times," he replied and I understood why I liked him. He wasn't really shy. He had a more mature way about him, a quieter, far more self-assured manner than most of the boys in my class. He was a contender for valedictorian, only half a percentage point separating him from Judy McCarthy, a girl the other students called "Dot Com" because of her computer-like brain and zero personality.

Barry tried his best to reassure me as we drove to my house. He talked about duck hunters who lost track of time, uncles of his who went to such out-of-the-way places for their secret spots it took half a day to get back.

"Maybe your dad just met up with one of the old-timers here who took him to his special pond or whatever. Some of these guys travel hundreds of miles to shoot a duck."

"You don't go hunting?" I asked him.

He shook his head.

"I fish a little, but I've never been into guns. My father wishes I was. He'd like me to go with him, but I never took to it. Bugs, mud, ugh," he said, and I had my first smile since Daddy hadn't arrived at five.

I thanked Barry and got out of his car quickly when we pulled into my driveway. I could see that Daddy's Jeep was still not there.

"I'll call you," Barry shouted as I hurried to the door.

I waved back at him and practically lunged into the house.

Mommy was in the living room staring at the wall. I caught my breath and waited.

"I phoned the police and it was just as I expected. They told me he'd have to be gone longer for them to consider it any sort of police matter. I asked how long and the dispatcher said longer. He wouldn't give me a specific time."

She lifted her hands, palms up.

"What do we do?"

"What can we do, Mommy? We wait," I said and sat beside her.

She took my hand and rocked a bit and then she leaned against me and we both sat there, our hearts pounding as one, waiting in silence.

"Put on the television set," Mommy said after a while. "I need something to distract me."

I did. We gazed at the picture, heard the voices of the actors, but it all ran together. Near midnight, Mommy fell asleep beside me. I rose to turn off the television set when I saw the car headlights pulling into our driveway. My heart did flip-flops. *Daddy,* I thought. *Finally.*

But when I stepped up to the window, I saw it wasn't Daddy. It was a police car, with the emblem on the side identifying it as a Georgia State Police vehicle. Two officers stepped out, put on their hats, and walked toward our front door. For a moment, I couldn't move; I couldn't breathe. I just watched them approaching. Then I turned to Mommy. I thought I said, "Mommy," but she didn't stir and I wasn't sure if I had spoken or shouted in my own mind.

The sound of the door buzzer made her eyelids flutter. The policemen pressed the buzzer again and Mommy opened her eyes, looked at me, and sat up.

"Was that our front door?"

"Yes, Mommy," I said. I couldn't swallow.

"Well, who would be here at this hour?"

I glanced out the window and then back at her.

"It's the police, Mommy."

"The police?"

She smothered a cry. She seemed frozen. Her hand hovered near her throat. Something horrible exploded in my heart just watching her reactions.

"Go," she finally managed to utter.

I went quickly to the door and opened it. They had

their hats off again. Both looked so tall and impressive, larger than life, beyond reality, like two characters who had emerged from the televison program we were barely watching.

"Is this the home of Charles Wallace?" the slightly taller one on the right asked me.

"Yes."

"Is Mrs. Wallace here?"

"Yes." I'm glad they didn't ask another question. I didn't think I could say more.

They stepped in and I backed up. The second patrolman closed thc door behind him.

"May we speak with her?" the first patrolman asked me.

I nodded and went to the living room doorway. They followed.

"Mrs. Charles Wallace?" he asked.

Mommy nodded—slightly, stiffly. Quickly, I went to her side and she reached up for my hand.

The patrolman approached us. In the light his face looked pale, his eyes two ebony marbles.

"I'm sorry, ma'am, but your husband appears to have been in a serious hunting accident. A few hours ago, a farmer out in Granville Lake called the local police to report a row boat with a man slumped in it."

A long sighed escaped from Mommy's choked throat. She swayed and would have fallen forward, if I hadn't held tightly to her hand.

"The patrolman on the scene reported what looked like a gun accident, ma'am. Searching for identification, he came up with your husband's license and other items. He had a fatal wound in his chest area. I'm sorry," the patrolman said.

"My husband...is...dead?" Mommy asked. She had to hear the definite words.

"I'm very sorry," he replied, nodding. "It's too early to tell, but preliminary examination suggests he was killed instantly and some time before he was discovered."

"I called the police to report him being very late," Mommy said, as if that should have prevented it. "They told me I would have to wait longer."

The patrolman nodded.

"Yes, ma'am. What we have here is an unattended death, ma'am, so there is a mandatory autopsy."

My legs finally gave out on me and I crumpled to the sofa and sat beside her. Mommy just stared at the two patrolmen.

"Maybe there's someone you should call," the second patrolman directed to me.

I shook my head.

"Someone will be here in the morning to tell you more," the first patrolman continued. "Is there anything we can do for you at the moment?"

Mommy shook her head.

I didn't feel myself. I thought I had turned into pure air and a breeze would come along and simply scatter me everywhere. My daddy was dead? He wasn't coming home for his duck dinner. He was never coming home again. Mommy and I were alone forever.

The second patrolman stepped forward and held out

a plastic bag with Daddy's personal things in it. I saw his wallet, his watch, and his wedding ring. Mommy just looked up at it. I reached out and took it.

"We located his vehicle about a mile upstream," the patrolman said after I took the bag. "After we examine it, we'll have it brought back."

"This is very unfortunate, ma'am. Did your husband go out by himself, do you know, or did he go with someone else?" the first patrolman asked softly.

Suddenly, I felt we really were in a television movie. The police were trying to determine if Daddy's death was truly accidental.

"Himself," Mommy managed to utter.

"You're positive, ma'am?"

"He didn't go out with anyone," I said sharply.

The patrolman nodded.

"Was he upset when he left today?" he continued.

"Upset?" My mother smiled. "No, not Charles. Not Charles, never upset."

They stood there silently. What were they after? What were they trying to say?

"What could have happened?" I asked.

The second patrolman shook his head.

"He could have tripped and accidentally discharged the gun," he suggested. "It's not the most uncommon thing to happen."

"It's never wise to go out alone," the first patrolman said, as if we could learn an important lesson from this.

"Tripped?" my mother muttered.

"Well, we did find he was drinking some, ma'am.

There was a bottle of bourbon in the boat. Guns and whiskey just don't mix," he added. Another valuable lesson.

Mommy just stared up at him. I looked at the floor. The words were all jumbling in my mind, stacking up and sprawling out like some product on an assembly line in the Lewis Foundry going awry.

"You're sure there's nothing we can do for you?" the second patrolman asked.

Mommy shook her head, her eyes so glassy they looked fake.

"Please accept our condolences, ma'am."

They stood there a moment and then both turned and walked out the door. We heard them open the front door and close it behind them. I looked down at the plastic bag containing Daddy's things in my hand. Mommy followed my eyes and stared at it, too.

She reached out and took the bag, plucking the ring gently from the bag and turning it in her fingers.

"Charles," she said and she started to sob, deep rasping sobs emerging from her throat, but no tears yet from her eyes. It was all taking hold slowly, but firmly, the realization, the reality that this was not some nightmare. This had just happened.

I saw the words and the thoughts forming in her eyes.

Her husband was gone.

I took a deep breath. I had to let reality in, too. I had to let the thought take shape.

My daddy was gone.

3

Secrets

After my daddy's death, the nightmares and bleak thoughts that had shadowed our lives for so long finally took more solid shapes and crossed over the line between the darkness and the light. One discovery after another descended on our small, fragile world with the force of a sledgehammer. Mommy made the shocking discovery that Daddy had neglected to pay his life insurance premiums. Somewhere along the rough and uneven line of our lives, he had simply overlooked it, or in his inimitable fashion had decided, why worry about dying?

Thinking back now, I realized we never spoke much about death in our house. My father had become so estranged from his parents that he didn't attend his own father's funeral. He did go to his mother's, but he didn't take me or my mother along. It was almost just another business trip because he attached an interview with a prospective new employer to his itinerary and when he returned had nothing to say about his relatives.

My mother's parents had long since disowned her and put all their attention and love into her younger brother and sister. She tried to restore a relationship, but my grandfather was a stubborn, unforgiving man whose reply and philosophy was "You made your bed. Now lie in it."

I had only vague memories of both of them, and the one picture Mommy had of her father was of him staring at the camera, almost daring it to capture his image. Mommy told me he didn't believe in smiling for pictures because it made him look insubstantial and foolish, and he hated being thought anything but important. Looking at him in the picture frightened me so much, I had nightmares.

Neither he nor my grandmother responded to the announcement of my father's death and more importantly didn't offer any assistance. It compounded my mother's sorrow and laid another heavy rock on her chest.

The only time I could actually recall my father talking about death was when he said, why talk about it?

"As I see it, there are things over which you have some control and things over which you don't, Rose. Just forget about the ones you don't. Pretend they don't exist and it won't bother you," he told me.

However, for us, that translated into all sorts of big problems—beginning with no money for a real funeral, a grave site, or a tombstone. When Mommy lamented about these things, I wondered why she had permitted it to happen, too. Why hadn't she insisted on facing realities? Why hadn't she seen to it that these things were addressed? Why did she bury her head in the sand Daddy poured around us? I wanted to scream at her, demanding to know why she had put up with all of this irresponsibility.

But how do you ask such questions and say such hard things to a woman who looked likc she was being dragged over hot coals by a cruel and indifferent Fate? Was there any way to have such a sensible conversation with someone who looked stunned, who barely could eat or talk or dress herself in the morning? She was always a woman who paid attention to her appearance, and now, she didn't care how washed-out and haggard she looked.

Fortunately for us, Mr. Kruegar decided he would pay Daddy's salary for two more months and help with the funeral costs. Apparently, he really did like Daddy and enjoyed his company at the dealership. As soon as the news of Daddy's death was out, Mr. Kruegar was the first one to come calling, and that was when he made all these offers.

"We got a lot of new business out of sponsoring you in the beauty contest," he told me as we all sat in our living room. It was so still and quiet, it did seem as if the world had been put on pause. "I'm glad your father asked me to do it."

I simply stared at him. *How could he talk about something like that at this horrible time?* I wondered.

He smiled at Mommy. She nodded, but she looked

like she would nod at anything, even if he merely cleared his throat.

"You know, next month is Kruegar's twenty-fifth anniversary. I'm thinking of having a big celebration. Refreshments, balloons, little mementos to give out, special discounts on the new cars and used cars, stuff like that. I'm going to have the local television network there and a radio station broadcasting from my site. I'd like you to come down and be one of my hostesses," he told me. "Maybe you could wear that beauty contest swimsuit and do that hula-hula dance you did. You'll be on television.

"I'll pay you a hundred dollars a day that weekend," he added.

Mommy raised her eyebrows and looked at me.

"I don't feel much like parading around in a bathing suit and dancing, Mr. Kruegar."

"Oh, I know that. Not now, but next month. Give it some thought, okay? I'd like to do what I can to help you people. I'll miss him. Great guy, great salesman. Broke a record in March, you know. I gave him that thousand dollar bonus for it."

He turned to Mommy, but she shook her head and I realized Daddy had never told her. I wondered why. I think Mr. Kruegar realized it, too, because he suddenly looked embarrassed and made his excuses to leave.

Some of my school friends came to visit and a few of the women Mommy had gotten to know and be friendly with brought baskets of fruit and flowers, some coming with their husbands, but most coming alone. Everyone wanted to know what we were going to do now, but few came right out and actually asked. I think they were afraid she might ask them for help.

Mommy was still considering going to work at the insurance company. We were in very bad financial condition, even with the two months' salary from Mr. Kruegar, because Daddy's income really came from commissions. We had little in a savings account and all our regular expenses loomed above and around us like big old trees threatening to crush us. In the evenings Mommy would sift through her possessions, considering what she could sell to raise some money. I felt so terrible about it, I offered to quit school and get a job myself. Of course, she wouldn't hear of it.

"You're so close to graduation, Rose. Don't be stupid."

"Well, how are we going to manage, Mommy?" I asked. "Bills are raining down around us like hail."

"We'll get by, somehow," she said. "Other people who suffer similar tragedies do, don't they?" she asked. It sounded too much like another of Daddy's promises floating in a bubble. I didn't reply, so her worrying continued.

At first she didn't tell me about her desperate pleas to her father, how she had belittled herself, and had accepted his nasty descriptions of her and of Daddy just to see if she could get him to advance her some money. In the end he relented and sent a check for a thousand dollars, calling it charity and saying since he would give this much to the Salvation Army, he would give this much to us. But he left it pretty clear that Mommy shouldn't ask him for another nickel. He told her he thought struggling, suffering, would be the best way for her to understand fully what a mess she had made with her life by not listening to him. It was more important for him to be right than generous and loving. When she finally broke down and told me all of it, she was shattered.

"I used to love him," she moaned as if that had been something of an accomplishment.

"Doesn't everyone love their fathers?" I asked.

"No," she said with her lips twisting and writhing with her pain. "There are some fathers you just can't love, for they don't want your love. They see showing emotion as weakness. I can't even remember him kissing me, whether it was good night, good-bye or on my birthday."

I decided Daddy had been correct about people like that: just cut them away as you would cut away so much swamp grass and keep your boat surging forward.

After the funeral and the period of bereavement, I returned to school. The night before I told Mommy that I had decided I was going to pretend Daddy wasn't gone. He was just on some sales trip. I was doing what he always did when he was faced with unpleasant events and problems, I decided. I was ignoring death. She became angry as soon as I finished telling her.

"I won't let you," she said. "You're not going to fall into the same traps I fell into, traps he set with his promises and his happy-go-lucky style. I let him mesmerize me, bedazzle and beguile me until I became too much like him. Look what it's gotten me!" she cried, her arms out. She turned to the mirror. "I'm old beyond my years because of all this worry and trouble.

"No, Rose. No. Your father is dead and gone. You must accept the truth, accept reality, and not live in some make-believe world as he did, and as I permitted myself to live in as well. Now we have to find ways to make the best of our lives without him.

"I'm sure wherever he is, he's belittling what happened to him and telling other souls to forget it. He's telling them they can't do anything about it, so just say, 'Whatever' and play your harp. He's probably looking for ways to move on to another heaven or hell for that matter, trying to get himself thrown out," she said. She smiled, but she was crying real tears, too.

I hugged her and promised not to ignore reality anymore. She forced me to confront it dramatically that night by helping her box all of his things, most of which she had decided to donate to charity.

"If we only made enough money to use it as a write-off," she muttered.

I hated folding his clothes and stuffing them in cartons. The scent of his cologne was still on most of them, and when the aroma entered my nostrils, it stirred pictures of him in my mind and the sound of his voice in my ears. I worked with Mommy, but I cried and sobbed, especially when I felt him twirling my hair and heard him reciting, "Your eyes are two diamonds. Your hair is spun gold. Your lips are rubies and your skin comes from pearls. My sweet Rose."

Closing the cartons was another way to say, "Good-bye, Daddy. Good-bye."

When we were nearly finished with the clothes in the closet, Mommy found a manila envelope under two boxes of old shoes in the far corner. She opened it and pulled out an eight by ten black and white photograph of a young woman. There was nothing written on the photograph or on the back of it and nothing else in the envelope.

"Who's this?" she wondered aloud, and I looked at the picture with her.

"You don't know?"

She shook her head.

The picture was of a woman who looked to be in her twenties. I couldn't tell the color of her hair, but it was either light brown or blond. She had a very pretty face with a button nose and sweet, full lips. There was a slight cleft in her chin. She had her hair cut and styled with strands sweeping up about her jawbone and she had high cheek bones with a smooth forehead. She looked very happy, as happy as someone who had found some great contentment in her life. There was that peacefulness in her eyes.

"She's no relative of mine, and I don't believe she's a relative of his," Mommy mused aloud. "Of course, she might be a cousin I never met, but why wouldn't he have ever shown me her picture?"

In the background we could just make out what looked like a large plantation house, a Greek revival with the grand pillars and style that were characteristic of some of the wealthier estates around Atlanta.

"Well," Mommy concluded with a deep sigh, "it doesn't surprise me that he never showed me the picture. Just another thing he didn't think mattered, I suppose."

She put it aside and we finished the work. I thought about the picture before I went to sleep and then I shrugged it off just the way Mommy had, thinking of Daddy's favorite word, "Whatever."

Barry Burton had called and visited me during the bereavement period, and he was there to greet me at my locker when I returned to school in the morning.

"Before you stumble on the gossip," he told me, "I want you to be prepared."

"What gossip?"

"There's talk your father deliberately killed himself, committed suicide."

I felt the hot tears of fury and pain forming under my lids. What right did anyone have making up such stories about him and why did they care anyway? Were they all so desperate for gossip? Or was it just the girls who despised me for being more attractive than they were? All these little jealousies were like termites eating away the foundation of any friendships in this place, I thought. I hated them all.

"If anyone does dare to say that in front of me..."

"Someone *will* do it just to get you upset, I'm sure," he warned. I could tell from his tone that he more than anticipated it. It hit me as sharply as a rock in the forehead when I gazed into his eyes.

"It's Paula, isn't it?" I asked.

He nodded.

"Why?"

He shrugged.

"She's been telling people about how it was when she went over to your house to pick you up that night, things she supposedly felt or heard."

"That's all a lie!"

He looked down.

"I think," he said softly, "that Ed was more interested in you than he was in her, and she learned that after we left them together. It didn't sit well with her. Remember English class and Shakespeare... 'Hell hath no fury like a woman scorned.' "

"This isn't English class and I don't care what Shakespeare or anyone else wrote. It's me and my family that's being scorned."

Was being attractive a curse or a blessing? Would I never have a close girlfriend because of that?

"I don't know where she got the idea that I cared for Ed Wiley anyway. If he has a crush on me, that's not my fault. I never encouraged him, Barry."

He smiled.

"I'm glad," he said. "Don't worry about it. Ignore her as best you can."

"Whatever," I said.

"Pardon?"

"Nothing. I've got to get to class."

"Right."

I know he stayed at my side as much as he could that day in hopes of preventing any problems, as well as because he really wanted to be with me. As it turned out, Paula was only a cowardly whisperer. She didn't have the courage to say anything aloud, especially anywhere near me, but I could tell from the way many of the students she had spoken to were looking at me and whispering that she had been spewing her verbal poison all around me. I was the one who eventually had to confront her, and confront her I did at the end of the day.

I walked up to her quickly as she was leaving the building and I scooped my arm under hers, pulling her to the side. She was so shocked she could barely resist. I knew she was athletic and more physical than I was, but I was driven by such rage, I think I could have broken her into pieces. She knew it, too, and didn't challenge me.

"I know you've been saying things about my family and my father, Paula. If you do it again, I'll rip out your tongue," I said so calmly, my eyes so fixed on hers, she could barely breathe.

She started to stutter an excuse and I put my hand flatly on her chest.

"Don't do it again," I said, digging the nail of my forefinger into her enough to make her back up. Then I walked away from her, my heart probably pounding louder and harder than hers.

Barry had seen me take her aside. He was waiting in his car to drive me home. After I got in, I told him what I had done and said and he laughed.

"You carried out a preventive strike. Good work," he told me. "You're going to be all right, Rose. You're going to be just fine."

After we pulled into my driveway, he gave me a quick kiss before I got out of his car.

"I'll call you later," he promised. "Maybe we can do something this weekend, huh?"

"Maybe," I said.

Somewhere very deep inside me, I sensed that grief would thin out no matter how thick and terrible it had been. I would never forget Daddy of course, but in time, he would grow distant. It would be as if we had let go of each other's hands and he had drifted back, back into the shadows, back into the vault of my memory.

Spirited by my return to normal life, I was hoping Mommy would be somewhat revived in spirit when I entered the house. Soon our lives would start to resemble some of what they had been, but the moment I set eyes on her, I knew it wasn't so, not yet.

"What's wrong, Mommy?" I asked. She was sitting on the sofa staring at a dark, mute television set.

"Mr. Weinberg hired someone else for the position at his insurance agency. He said he had made the decision before your father died or he would have given it to me. He looked sincere, even sick about it, but I don't want to be hired out of charity. I want to be hired because people believe I'm qualified.

"Now what?" she asked the dark television set. "I've got to search for something I'm suitable for, and what am I experienced to do? Work in a fast-food restaurant, find a counter-girl job in a department store? They pay bare minimum wages. We can't survive on that."

She turned to me, her eyes filled with rage as well as self-pity.

"When you get married, Rose, don't put all your faith and hope in your husband. I should have developed some skill, some talent, some means of being truly independent. Who would have expected I would have to start over like some teenager at this point in my life?" she moaned.

"I should just quit school and get a job, Mommy. I can finish my high school diploma later."

"No," she said. She pulled herself up and sucked back her tears of remorse. "I've got an appointment at social services. We're entitled to some money and if we have to..."

I didn't want to hear the word welfare, but it lingered on her lips. I could practically see its formation.

"I'll at least look for a weekend job, Mommy. Please."

She sighed and shook her head.

"Where's your father when I need him to say his famous 'Whatever' now?"

She rose with great effort and started out.

"I'll start fixing something for dinner. Go do your homework or call a girlfriend and jabber on the phone, Rose. I don't want to see you lose your chance to live, too," she added and shuffled off.

What a sad sight she made. It left a lump of lead in

my chest. I had to swallow hard to keep the tears back. Daddy had let us down so badly. Even the memory of his smile was losing its shine for me.

But I had no idea how much it would.

Not until the door buzzer sounded an hour later.

I was on my way down to set the table and see what else I could do to help Mommy, so I went right to the door and opened it. A stylish woman who looked to be in her late forties or early fifties stood there. She wore a navy blue three-button suit and had her reddish-blond hair done in a square cut with the front ends at a slant. She wore medium high heels and looked to be about five feet four or five. Her aquamarine eyes scanned me so intensely, I felt as if I was under a spotlight. She didn't smile, but her eyes were filled with interest and curiosity. Although I was absolutely sure I had never seen her before, there was something vaguely familiar about her. It came to me before I spoke. She had the same slight cleft in her chin as did the mysterious woman in the photo Mommy had found in the closet when we were packing Daddy's things for charity.

"Am I correct in assuming that this is the home of Charles Wallace?" she asked in perfectly shaped consonants and vowels, despite her thick Georgian accent.

"Yes," I replied. I looked past her and saw the late-model black town car with a chauffeur in our driveway. He sat with perfect posture, staring stiffly ahead like a manikin.

"I would like to see Mrs. Wallace," she said.

"Who's there, Rose?" Mommy called from the kitchen.

"My name is Charlotte Alden Curtis," the elegant woman told me.

I stepped back and she entered. She looked at our hallway, the walls, the ceiling as if she was deciding if anything was contaminated.

"There's someone here to see you, Mommy," I called back.

"You are the daughter," the woman said, nodding. "Yes," she added as she confirmed something in her mind after studying me a bit longer. "His daughter."

Mommy came out of the kitchen, wiping her hands on a dishtowel.

"Who is it?" she asked as she approached us.

"My name is Charlotte Alden Curtis, Mrs. Wallace," she said and looked like she expected that would mean something to Mommy.

"Oh," Mommy said, looking to me to see if I knew any more. I shook my head slightly. "Well, how can I help you?" Mommy asked.

"I have come here to tell you exactly how you can help me, Mrs. Wallace," Charlotte Alden Curtis said. "May we sit and talk someplace? I am not accustomed to holding court in a hallway."

Mommy just stared at her a moment and then snapped her head to the right, realizing the woman was waiting for a reply.

"Oh, yes, of course. Right this way," Mommy said, leading her to our living room. She nodded at the sofa where I had left a magazine and I hurried ahead to get it and pick up the glass of lemonade I had left on the center table. "Please," Mommy said nodding at the chair across from the sofa.

Charlotte Alden Curtis considcred it as if she might turn down the suggestion and then sat slowly, leaning back and looking up at us. I realized we were both gaping. Mommy nudged me and we both sat on the settee.

"What is this about?" Mommy quickly inquired.

"Your husband," Charlotte replied with gunshot speed.

"My husband? Oh." Mommy's body relaxed in a slight slump. "Does he owe you money?"

Charlotte Alden Curtis lifted her eyebrows and pressed her shapely lips together so firmly, her otherwise narrow cheeks bubbled.

"I am hardly a bill collector," she said. "Are you accustomed to bill collectors in designer clothes?"

"Well, who are you? What do you want?" Mommy demanded somewhat more firmly.

"I am Angelica Alden's older sister, and what I want is justice, not money," she answered. "It has taken me some time to locate y'all. Your husband moved you people so often, apparently. Of course, I understand why.

"My nephew Evan is something of a computer wiz these days. The computer is actually a godsend when it comes to Evan. He's confined to a wheelchair as a result of a spinal deformity that affected his legs. It was

Evan who finally tracked y'all after I pleaded with him to do so. He never wanted to find your husband. I'm sure he could have done it way before this," she added. She paused and looked around the living room with the same expression of utter contempt.

"I understand he's dead," she added.

"My husband passed away recently, yes," Mommy said. "Why did you want to locate him if it has nothing to do with money?"

"Passed away," Charlotte muttered instead of answering. "He passed away some time ago, as far as I am concerned."

"What is it you want, Miss—or is it Mrs. Curtis?" Mommy asked, her voice now ringing with annoyance as well as impatience.

"It's Mrs. Curtis. I am a widow. I lost my husband ten years ago. Congestive heart failure. He was pounds and pounds overweight, a heavy smoker and drinker, and stubborn as the proverbial mule. He had other self-destructive habits as well, but I won't get into that now.

"Suffice it to say he left me well-to-do, wealthy enough to care for my wayward sister and her child all these years. My sister and I raised her boy. You can just imagine what a burden that has been. It's hard enough to raise teenagers these days," she said, looking at me, "much less a teenager with special needs."

Mommy said nothing. She and I just stared and waited.

"A little over a year ago, my sister Angelica passed

away, too. She was in a brutal car accident, a head-on collision caused by a drunken redneck who still walks the earth and, I am sure, still overindulges himself in every way possible. One of those nephews of a judge with some influence. You know how those things can be," she added.

"Her death had a very heavy impact on Evan, of course, but an even heavier one on me."

Mommy nodded in sympathy, but still waited tensely to understand the point of this visit.

"Well, what exactly can we do for you, Mrs. Curtis? At the moment we can barely do enough for ourselves," Mommy said.

"I know just how true that is. What I would like, what I'm proposing, is that you and your daughter come live with me and help me take care of Evan," Charlotte Alden Curtis finally said.

Mommy smiled with confusion.

"Pardon me?"

"I can't bear the burden any longer and I shouldn't have to bear it alone," Charlotte continued. "It's aging me faster than I would like, to say the least."

"I'm sorry for you, Mrs. Curtis. However..."

"I know you're in financial turmoil, Mrs. Wallace. Once I learned where y'all had gone this time, I had my attorneys make inquiries. You can't keep up the rent even for a house like this," she added, looking about our home as if it was nothing more than a tent.

"That might be true," Mommy said, her indignation rising like mercury in a thermometer, "however, I am not in the habit of having strangers come to my home to make demands on us just because we're in a temporary crisis."

"Temporary," Charlotte said, smiling and shaking her head. "Why delude yourself, Mrs. Wallace? Unless you find a daddy for Rose here, you'll always be in a monetary crisis. You have no work skills, no significant record of employment, and I don't believe you are the type who wants to do menial labor. You're still an attractive and relatively young woman, as I am. You shouldn't be burdened with the responsibility of providing the basic necessities of life for yourself and your daughter. You have a lot of good living to do, beautiful things to enjoy. Just as I do."

Mommy started to speak, but stopped and looked at me. I shook my head again.

Mommy shook hers and started to laugh.

"Really, Mrs. Curtis, I do feel sorry for you, but why should we even entertain the idea of moving in with you to help you care for a disabled child? I have no experience with that sort of thing, either, and Rose certainly doesn't. I must say, Mrs. Curtis, your searching for us and coming here to make such a request makes no sense to me and..."

"It will," Charlotte said confidently.

"Really? Why?"

"Evan is your husband's child," she replied coolly.

The words seemed to bounce off me, but Mommy

looked as if all the air had gone out of her lungs. She turned as white as rice.

"What did you say?"

"I said, Evan is your husband's child, your daughter's half-brother," she added, looking at me.

Mommy started to shake her head. Charlotte opened her pocketbook and took out two envelopes.

"This first one contains a letter your husband wrote to my poor sister, making pathetic excuses for himself and his behavior with her and offering to pay for her to have an abortion. That offer came too late, not that Angelica would have agreed to do it. She was a helpless romantic. You'll recognize his handwriting and his signature, I'm sure.

"This second letter also contains a check, an even more pathetic attempt to buy off his guilt, I suppose. It's for a thousand dollars."

Daddy's bonus, I thought as she handed both envelopes to Mommy. She took them, but she looked like she didn't have the strength to hold them. I watched her take out the letter from the first one and read it. She put it down and looked at the second and at the check.

"Well?"

Mommy's eyes looked frozen over.

"Mommy?" I said. She handed me the letters and the check and I read it all quickly, my heart feeling as if it had stopped altogether and evaporated. My chest felt that empty, that hollow.

"I don't know what to say, Mrs. Curtis. You can see

that this is all a very big surprise to me," Mommy managed.

"Well, I would hope so. I don't know how any woman could live with a man knowing he had seduced a young, impressionable woman, made her pregnant, and then deserted her, especially after she gave birth to an imperfect child, his child, who needs such special care.

"In the early years, I paid for all the nursing and the rehabilitation and the tutors. Angelica lived for the longest time under the illusion that your husband would eventually come to her assistance and to the aid of his own child. He had her believing they would live happily ever after.

"It broke her heart to see how he avoided her as much as possible, sometimes never contacting her at all for months and months. The foolish girl actually prevented herself from finding new and substantial relationships with other men, more responsible and decent men, because your husband kept her on the edge of her chair with his 'very soon now' sort of lies.

"Well, she's gone and there's just the two of us, the poor child and myself, and frankly, I am not ready to live like some nun, sacrificing all of the finer things in life. As you can see, I am still young enough to enjoy the fruits of my husband's fortune.

"Now that you are destitute, it makes absolute sense for you to come to my home and help me care for Evan. I have a sizable fortune, a large old plantation house just outside of Atlanta. I have servants, of course, but the boy needs more than a maid and an occasional nurse's visit. He needs family."

"Family?" Mommy asked, a smile of incredulity on her face.

"Well, other than myself, some cousins on my side, and your husband's relatives, your daughter is the only immediate family he has.

"Frankly, Mrs. Wallace, I do believe you have some responsibility here."

"I do?"

"Your husband bears the guilt. If your husband runs up a monetary debt, you are still responsible for it as well, aren't you? His death doesn't forgive all that. Certainly a child is at least as valuable and as important as some money."

Mommy's mouth opened and closed. She shook her head.

"As I see this," Charlotte said, gazing around the living room, "I'm offering you a way out of this disastrous mess your husband has left you."

"You want me to become a mother to your sister's child?" Mommy finally was able to ask.

"And your husband's child and your own child's half-brother," Charlotte replied. She pulled herself up. "In point of fact, my dear, you have more reason to be a surrogate mother to him than I have."

Mommy sat back.

"Why don't we plan on your visiting tomorrow? I'll send my car for you. Perhaps when you see where you would live and what you would enjoy, you'll lose any hesitation."

She rose and looked at me.

"Evan would so much enjoy having someone his own age around him. He's had minimal contact with other teenagers, and that's why he's so tied to his computer. You could do a great deal for him, my dear. You could help repair the terrible injury your father visited upon my family and my poor dead sister. Shall we say about ten A.M.?" she asked Mommy.

Mommy looked incapable of replying.

"My mother and I will discuss all this, Mrs. Curtis," I said. "It's all quite a shock."

"Yes, but imagine the shocks I've experienced," she retorted and started out. I rose to follow her to the door. After she opened it, she turned back to me.

"No one knows about this disgrace and no one needs to know. As far as the inquiring public goes, you and your mother will be hired to help me manage. Should you refuse, I would have to speak with my attorneys to determine what course of action would best benefit poor Evan."

"What's that supposed to mean?" I asked.

"There is paternal responsibility."

"We have nothing, Mrs. Curtis. You know that already," I said sharply.

"Yes, I know. I suppose I would have to find some sort of institutionalized setting for Evan. Another burden of suffering piled on his poor soul, and all because your father turned his charms on my poor sister. Remember your Bible, my dear. The sins of the father are visited on the heads of his children."

She turned and stepped out.

"Someone will call you tonight to confirm the pickup tomorrow morning," she concluded and walked to her waiting car.

I watched her vehicle drive off, the sight of it lingering like a vivid new nightmare.

4

The Mansion

Mommy was still sitting exactly where we had left her, the same dumbfounded expression on her face. After a moment she turned to me.

"Do you believe all that?" She looked down at the letters in her hand and the check. "How could he have done this? How could he have kept such a dark secret? Did he treat this with the same nonchalance he treated everything else in our lives? Did he not expect that it would come back at him someday?"

I lowered myself to a chair and stared at the floor. Like a tickle that turned into a scratch, a horrible gnawing thought made its way to the top of my thoughts. Slowly, I raised my eyes to Mommy.

"Some people think Daddy might have deliberately killed himself, Mommy. Do you think this makes it more likely to be true?"

The idea dawned on her, too, but when it came to her, it was more like a slap in the face.

She shook her head, but she started to cry. I leaped from my chair to embrace her and the two of us sat there on the settee, rocking each other, tears streaking down both our faces. Finally, she took a deep breath and sat back.

"What does that woman really want?" she asked me.

"I don't know, Mommy."

She thought a moment.

"She did look very rich," she said, and gazed with haunted eyes at our small, dark, and tired living room. "Maybe we should see what it's really all about."

"You mean, go there?"

"Why not?" Mommy asked, rising. "When you're at the end of your rope and dangling, you look kindly on any hand reaching out to hold you up, Rose. Any hand," she concluded and returned to the kitchen.

Neither of us had much of an appetite, but we both ate mechanically so the other would. Every once in a while, Mommy would choke back a sob and shake her head while she muttered about Daddy.

"I almost do feel sorrier for that poor dead girl than I do for myself. I can see how she could easily be charmed and persuaded by your father. He enjoyed spreading his illusions and dreams. He was the Pied Piper of Fantasyland, leading us all down the road to popped bubbles."

She thought a moment, and then jumped up from the table and went upstairs. Moments later she returned with that black and white photograph she had found in the closet and put it on the table. We both stared down at the young woman again, Mommy nodding.

"This must be Angelica. I can see the resemblances to Charlotte, can't you?"

I had to admit I could.

"Why did he keep her picture in our house?" she wondered aloud.

She shook her head at my blank stare.

"You don't have to say it. I can see it in your face. Why should I look for logic in a man who never paid attention to logic?" She took a deep breath and gazed at the picture again. "I'm not going to look for ways to deny it, to pretend it didn't happen, Rose."

Just then, as if some great power was listening in on our conversation and arranging for everything to happen, the phone rang. Mommy went to it and I listened.

"Yes," she said, "we will be ready." She nodded as she listened and then she hung up. "The car will be here at ten," she said. "We might as well learn all of it. You'll have to miss a day of school, Rose."

"Okay, Mommy."

It saddened me, but when I looked down at the photograph, it seemed as if the girl in the picture was smiling more.

When Barry called me later that evening, I was tempted to tell him about it all, but my embarrassment and my fears that it would fan the fires of nasty gossip, especially regarding the cause of Daddy's death, kept me from uttering a word of truth. I told him I would go to the movies with him on Friday, but not to be concerned about my being absent tomorrow. I said I had some important family business that needed to be attended to and left it at that.

"I'll miss you," he said. It added the touch of warmth I desperately needed to keep the chill from my cringing heart.

The town car was there promptly at ten the next morning. There was only the driver waiting. He was a tall, dark man with military-style posture. He introduced himself simply as Ames and opened the doors for Mommy and me. We got in and moments later, we were headed toward Atlanta.

"It's really only about thirty minutes from here," he explained. "If you'd like any candy, ma'am, there's some in a dish behind you."

"No, thank you," Mommy said.

He was quiet the remainder of the journey until we were approaching the driveway of the Curtis mansion.

"We're here," he announced.

Two sprawling great oak trees stood like sentinels at the scrolled cast-iron gate, which was fastened to two columns of stone. It opened before us and we drove on to see a truly magnificent two-story house with four Doric pillars, a full height entry porch, and elaborate cornices. Mommy looked at me with amazement in her eyes.

"Is this a house or a museum?" she muttered.

The grounds spread out around the house for what looked like miles. I saw two men trimming bushes and another riding a lawn mower. In the distance a line of trees formed a solid wall of green under the blue horizon. I had seen houses and land like this before, of course, but I had never known anyone who actually lived in such a home.

The driver brought us to the front steps. We got out slowly, both of us so busy filling our eyes with the sights and the immensity of the estate, neither of us saw the front door open.

A short, plump woman wearing a white apron and a blue maid's uniform waited. We started up the stairway. Instinctively I moved closer to Mommy.

"Right this way, please," the maid said, and we entered behind her.

"A museum," Mommy whispered again.

Before us was a curved stairway with a shiny, thick mahogany balustrade; on the walls were large oil paintings of beautiful country settings, lakes, and meadows, all done in vibrant colors, many, it seemed, by the same artist. Vases on marble-topped tables and glass cases filled with expensive-looking figurines, crystals, and the like lined the hallway, the floor of which was Italian marble.

"Please wait here," the maid said, showing us into a sitting room with elegant gold-trimmed velvet curtains over the windows, a plush white rug, and oversized pieces of furniture including what looked like a brass statue of an Egyptian queen. The room was so large, I thought we could put most of our present house in it. "Mrs. Curtis will be here in a moment. Would you like anything to drink—a cold lemonade, juice, soda?"

"Lemonade," Mommy said.

"Yes," I added.

"Very good," the maid said and left us.

Mommy strolled around the immense room looking at the artifacts, the paintings, and the antique furnishing.

"A woman who owns all this could *hire* a family for the boy," Mommy declared. "Why would she need us?"

"Because hired help is not family," we heard from behind us and turned to see Charlotte Alden Curtis enter.

She looked as elegant and stylish as the day before, albeit a little younger in a cream-colored pantsuit. Gold earrings dangled from her lobes. She wore a gold necklace and watch that looked bejeweled enough for the queen of Saudi Arabia.

"I'm very happy you decided to come. It was a wise decision for yourself and your daughter," she told Mommy.

"We came to see what this was all about, Mrs. Curtis. It doesn't mean we've agreed to anything."

"Let's agree on one thing immediately: that you'll stop calling me Mrs. Curtis and I'll stop calling you Mrs. Wallace. My name is Charlotte and I'm not much older than you are, Monica—a month, matter of fact. Please," she said, indicating the sofa. She sat across from us.

The maid brought in the lemonades, asked her if she wanted anything, which she didn't, and then quickly left.

"This one, Nancy Sue, has been with me for three years, a record of sorts for a household servant these days. Things," she said with a great sigh, "are not what they were. You have to work harder to find the quality of help my parents and my husband's parents once enjoyed. The grand style is still out there, but it takes more work to attain it."

Grand style? We were simply hoping to survive and she was talking about the quality of servants.

"Let me begin by telling you that I have already spoken with the headmistress of the school I would have Rose attend here. She assures me she would make Rose's transition easy, accommodating her needs and helping her to adjust rapidly."

That's right, I thought. *I would have to leave school, and right at the end of only the first quarter of my senior year!* I turned sharply to Mommy.

"That would be a major problem," she said.

"Oh, no, no, believe me, it won't. If need be, the school would provide a special tutor just to help her adjust. We'll arrange for it no matter what it should cost. I'm sure it won't be any sort of obstacle."

"The work isn't everything. She's made friends, become..."

"Friends?" Charlotte pulled herself up and turned to me. "You can certainly keep any friends, any real friends you've made, but imagine being able to invite them here as compared to where you are now," she said with naked arrogance.

"I don't have many friends," I admitted. I thought about the nasty rumors being spread about Daddy and what I had to face when I returned. "Not many at all."

She smiled.

"You will here, my dear, I'm sure. You are an exceptionally attractive young lady. Boys will flock to you as bears to honey, but I bet you know that already."

I started to protest how that wasn't really my biggest concern, but she rose to end the topic.

"Let me show you the house," she suggested. "I am rather proud of it. It's an authentic Greek revival."

She started out and we followed down the hallway to a large dining room with a table that seated twenty. There was a second, more informal sitting room, an office that looked unused, and of course, the large kitchen.

When we stepped into the hall again, I heard Charlotte say, "Good," under her breath and I turned to look to my right.

Evan had wheeled himself out of his room. Mommy and I gazed at him. He had Daddy's shade of hair, and it was down around his shoulders. The bangs were too long, so that he had to part the strands to prevent them obstructing his vision. He wore a pair of jeans and a T-shirt that said Evan Dot Com, something he took off his computer, and a pair of leather slippers with no socks.

"I'm happy you've decided to come out to meet everyone, Evan," Charlotte said. "This is your sister, Rose, and her mother, Monica."

He stared at us a moment, and then he turned the chair sharply and wheeled himself back into his room without a word.

Charlotte groaned.

"Oh, dear. You can see what it's like. He can be so

difficult, withdrawn. I try so hard to teach him common courtesies, but he has gotten so he is far more comfortable in the society of computers and machines than he is in the company of people. The poor boy avoids all human contact. That's what I am hoping you will correct, dear," she said to me. "He hasn't a single friend. Oh, he has all those names he talks to over the computer, but that's hardly being in any sort of society."

"How is his health?" Mommy asked.

"Aside from his problem with his legs, he is a healthy young man. He doesn't get out long enough to catch anything," she added as if that was something to regret. "I have to have the barber come here when he will permit it and then he won't let the man do much more than snip an inch or so here and there, and you should see what it's like to get him to go to the dentist or to his doctor. The only thing that gets him excited is shopping at one of those electronic stores, and he doesn't do that very much anymore either, because he's able to do it all over the computer. Sometimes, I think he is turning into a computer."

She sighed again.

"Please," she said, "follow me."

She led us up the stairs to show us what would be our rooms.

The room she said would be Mommy's had a queen-sized cherry four-poster bed, a sitting area with a fireplace and a television set in a matching wood cabinet. The room had its own bathroom. There were two large windows facing south with pretty flower-patterned curtains. The floor was a rich maple wood with an area rug. The room looked warm, comfortable, and very inviting. Charlotte pointed out all the closet space.

When Mommy said she had hardly enough to fill half of it, Charlotte replied, "Well, you will be buying more clothes, Monica. I want you to be very stylish and in fashion. My hope is you and I will become good friends and go to many social affairs together. You'll be the sister I've lost," she said. "I'm looking forward to that," she added with such sincerity, Mommy had to look at me with surprise. I didn't know what to say or do to react.

"Let's look at Rose's room," Charlotte quickly continued.

The room she declared would be mine was right across from Mommy's and just as large, also with its own bathroom and small sitting area with a television set on a stand. There was a queen-sized light oak bed with what looked like handmade quilts. Above it was a ceiling fan, and there were two large windows with curtains that matched the quilts. The area rug was somewhat larger. This, too, looked very warm and comfortable.

"You can have your own phone, of course," Charlotte told me. "I'll have it set up with your private number."

What could I say? The room was easily twice, if not three times, the size of my present room, and I didn't have my own bathroom like I would here.

"This was my sister's room," she added. She turned to me to see my reaction.

I felt a quickened heartbeat and looked at the room again.

"Of course, all of her things are gone. I gave most of it away and stored some of her personal things in the attic.

"There are two more guest bedrooms and the master bedroom up here and a guest bedroom downstairs," she said. "As you can see, plenty of room, too much for just little old me and poor crippled Evan now."

Mommy looked at me again and then turned to her.

"What is it you expect from us exactly, Charlotte? You have a maid who cooks your meals and cleans your home. You have a chauffeur. You have all you need to look after you and the house. I understand why you want a companion for Evan, but what would I do?"

Charlotte nodded and sat on the chair to the right of the bed. Her face softened, her eyes warming.

"That's all true, Monica, but when I leave here, I can't help feeling I'm deserting him. This is such a big house. It can feel so empty sometimes, so cold. With you and Rose here, too, there will be so much added warmth. I am hoping it will eventually bring Evan out and what my poor dead sister wanted so much for him will finally take place. Does that help you understand? Doesn't it make sense?"

Nodding slowly, Mommy looked around the room and at me, her mind obviously reeling with indecision, confusion.

"I am simply trying to get some good from all this tragedy and unhappiness," Charlotte said, seeing the same thing in Mommy's face. "Why should y'all continue to suffer? Why should Evan? Why should I when I have all this at my fingertips, more than I need?"

Mommy's head seemed to nod on its own and keep nodding.

"Let us talk about it, Charlotte," she offered.

"Oh, yes, dear," she replied with excitement. "Stay here. I'll see about lunch for all of us. Maybe Rose can entice poor Evan to come out and eat with people instead of a computer monitor," she said, rising quickly. "Feel free to look all around while I make the arrangements," she said and left us.

"I'm absolutely overwhelmed," Mommy said, reaching out to steady herself on the bedpost. "My head is spinning. Look at this place. It's like a five-star hotel. These rooms are so large and beautiful and the grounds...and you would attend a better school and she wants to buy me clothes..."

She paused and looked at me.

"What do you think, Rose?"

"I'm just as overwhelmed, Mommy. I don't know what to say. I don't want you getting sick with worry about our financial situation, a financial situation Daddy left us. I can also see how Charlotte is right and how she seems to need us. In a very twisted and strange way, this good thing is Daddy's doing, too."

Mommy nodded.

"Yes. I'll do it if you will," she said quickly. "I'm not so proud as to cause us to miss a chance to escape our misery and put so much of a burden on you."

I looked around at what would instantly become my new world, my new life. I couldn't stop my heart from pounding in anticipation, but what was it anticipating? Good things or bad?

"Let's look at all the rest of it," Mommy said suddenly, so filled with such excitement and joy, she shed the lines of worry and sorrow instantly.

Already she was looking younger, happier.

Charlotte Alden Curtis was right. She was either an angel of mercy.

Or an angel of temptation leading us to a deeper fall into unhappiness.

Mommy and I wandered through the house looking at the pictures of the Curtis and Alden families. We both lingered over pictures of Angelica. There were very few pictures of Evan, and in these he was always looking away or down and never smiling. I picked up the one on the grand piano and looked more closely at his face. It was only natural I suppose for me to look for resemblances to Daddy and to myself. I thought he definitely had Daddy's nose and jaw as well as his hair. In the pictures where I could have some view of his eyes, I thought they were his mother's eyes, and he did have his mother's slightly cleft chin.

Charlotte had her maid set up a small buffet lunch for us on the patio that was on the west side of the house and therefore soaked in warm sun. Soft blue umbrellas shaded the rolls, meats, and salads that were placed on the tables.

"Why don't you go to Evan," Charlotte asked me, "introduce yourself, and see if you can get him to join us for lunch?"

"I can't just go to his room," I said.

"Of course you can, dear. I want y'all to feel this house is your house immediately. Go on," she urged. "He won't bite. The worst thing he'll do is what he does often to me. He'll ignore you, pretend you're not there."

I looked at Mommy. She smiled some encouragement and I shrugged and started toward Evan's room. What a strange feeling came from realizing I was about to meet my brother for the first time. We shared the same father. We had similarities in our looks. Did that mean we might think alike, feel things the same way?

And what did he think of our father now? Did he hate him for what he had done to his mother, for helping to create him and then deserting him? Would his anger toward our father spread to me? Would he resent me and hate me no matter what I said or did?

I was actually trembling a bit when I approached the door to his room and knocked. I heard nothing, and thought perhaps I had knocked too softly, so I did it again much sharper, harder. Still, he didn't say come in or ask who it was. My third set of knocks actually opened the door. It wasn't closed tightly at all. It swung in and I looked at his room.

I hadn't been in many boys' rooms, but this certainly didn't look like any I would imagine. The walls were bare. There weren't any posters of sports heroes or movie and television stars or rock singers. The room itself resembled a cold, aseptic hospital room. There was a special bed made up with stark white sheets and pillow cases bounded by railings. Around the room were all sorts of therapeutic equipment.

At first I didn't think Evan was in the room, but when the door finished opening, I saw him staring at a computer monitor. He was also wearing headphones, which explained why he didn't hear my knocking. I saw that there was a microphone attached to the headphones and he was talking softly to someone. I thought I shouldn't interrupt him, but something told him I was in the doorway. Perhaps it was the shadow that came from the light behind me or maybe I was reflected in the glare of his computer screen. Whatever it was, he turned suddenly and looked at me, practically stabbing me with his furious eyes.

"I'm sorry," I began. "I knocked and then knocked again and your door just opened."

He said something into the microphone and slowly took off the headphones, placing it all in his lap.

"She tells me you're my sister," he said. His voice was deeper than I had expected and not unlike Daddy's. "My half-sister," he added.

"It seems to be so," I replied.

"She's trying to make it sound like half is better than none," he said. "That's not always true. Half a glass of cyanide isn't better than none; half a headache isn't better than none."

"I'm hardly poison and I don't think I give people headaches," I retorted. "Look, this is just as much a surprise for me and my mother as it is for you, believe me. More so," I added after a beat, "because, according to Charlotte, you've known about us for some time."

He stared, his eyes so unlike Daddy's. They were definitely his mother's eyes entirely—a deep blue, sapphire, but so penetrating, searching, and unmoving.

"I don't see why you and I have to suffer because of what others have done," I suggested.

His eyes brightened and softened.

"Oh, and how do I stop suffering?" he asked with a bit of an impish smile. "The best doctors haven't come up with an answer. Can you?"

"I'm not talking about that."

"What?" He was wheeling toward me. "What's that?"

"Your unfortunate condition," I said, nodding at him in the chair.

"Unfortunate condition. Yes, that's a good way to put it. Thank you. I used to call myself crippled."

" 'If you accept misery, you will be miserable,' Daddy used to say."

"Daddy? Daddy," he muttered. "You'll have to tell me about Daddy," he added, spitting the word like some profanity.

"I will," I said defiantly. "I'll tell you lots of things if you let me, but first you have to want me to. I'm not coming here begging you to be friends. I'd like to be friends, but if you don't want me to be your friend..."

"It's up to me. I know. She's always saying things

are up to me—as if I really had any control of anything," he complained.

"You do when it comes to our relationship."

He stared and then smiled.

"What's your real name?"

"That's my name."

"Rose? That's on your birth certificate?"

"Yes."

"What were they going to call the next child, Daffodil?"

"Very funny," I said. "Look, I'm hungry. There's a nice lunch out there. Do you want to have some lunch with me and talk sensibly, or do you want to shut yourself up in here and try to make us feel terrible, too?"

"That's a tough one," he said. He looked back at his computer. "I may have to go on a search engine to find the answer."

"Yes, well, when you do, come on out and join me," I said and started to turn away.

"Okay," he said.

"Okay?"

"Okay, I'm coming. Lead the way, *Rosie.*"

"I'm glad my name amuses you," I said and we started down the hallway, him wheeling himself alongside me. "I can push you, if you like," I said.

"Thanks, but this is all the exercise I'm getting today. My therapist isn't coming today."

"What were you doing on the computer? Who were you talking to?"

"I was in a chat room with other shut-ins. I created

the club. It's called Invalids Anonymous. We compare notes and depress each other."

"Doesn't sound like fun."

"We just got started. We'll find a way to have fun yet."

We reached the patio doors. Charlotte looked up. She and Mommy were seated at a table, talking and eating.

"Well, isn't this nice," she said.

"Yes," Evan said, "one big happy family."

He looked up at me with a half smile on his face, waiting for my reaction. In that split second, I saw the pain and the loneliness as well as the impishness in his eyes. He wasn't just crippled with a bone deformity. He was all twisted emotionally, full of anger and self-pity.

And yet I thought he was actually a very good-looking boy. He had the best of Daddy's features and his mother's. If some sparks of joy could light some happiness in those eyes, he would be very attractive, I concluded.

He seemed to be challenging me with his recalcitrant stare, daring me to do something that would help him, daring me to really be his sister, to be sincere and care about him. He looked like he expected me to flee, to turn away in disgust, but I didn't.

I smiled at him.

"This is my mother, Monica," I said. "She and my father named me Rose."

His eyes softened and filled with some humor.

"Hello, Evan," Mommy said.

He said hello politely.

"Can I get you a plate of food, Evan?" Charlotte asked him.

"No," he said sharply. He looked up at me. "I'd rather have Rose do it. By any other name, she'd smell as sweet."

Okay, I thought. *I'll play, too.*

"Too bad you don't," I threw down at him.

He seemed to wince, and then he laughed. The sound of it must have been alien to Charlotte. She dropped her mouth in amazement, and then looked at Mommy as I pushed Evan toward the food.

"I do believe this was meant to be," she said.

I would soon learn that what she meant by this and what we would interpret it to mean were two entirely different things.

5

Evan

After lunch, Evan allowed me to push him down the paths that wove through the gardens, ponds, and grounds around and behind the grand house. He said he wanted to show me his favorite places, but I sensed he wanted to get away from his aunt and Mommy to talk to me. I soon learned that Charlotte wasn't exaggerating when she characterized Evan as an introverted fifteen-year-old boy who had chained himself to his computer and who had minimal contact with the physical world around him. He reminded me of the allegory of Plato's Cave, one of the dialogues in Plato's *The Republic,* which my English teacher, Mr. Madeo, had made me read as an extra assignment just a few weeks ago.

In the allegory, people were living in an underground cave and chained so they could only look at the wall ahead of them. Above and behind them a fire burned so that everything that moved between the fire and them was thrown on the wall in the form of shadows. All they knew as real were the shadows and the echoes of sounds they heard and thought came from those shadows.

As Evan talked and described some of the things he did on his computer, the people he met and had gotten to know only over the Internet, I thought to myself that he was living in a cave—an electronic one, but still, a cave. His only friends were people he heard over his earphones and saw on his computer monitor. He traveled through the monitor and knew about exotic lands and people, but he had never really left the grounds of this estate. The only flowers he smelled or touched were the ones he could experience from his wheelchair trips down these paths. His world was populated solely by nurses, doctors, and other medical people, as well as a few servants and his tutor, Mrs. Skulnik, a fifty-eight-year-old retired math teacher who he said had a face like an old sock, so full of wrinkles it would take a tear two months to travel down to her chin.

"And she smells," he said, "like sour milk. I've told my aunt that I don't want her, but she says it's difficult to find someone else. I know she's not even trying.

"Maybe I don't need a tutor anyway," he suddenly thought aloud and looked up at me. "Maybe now that you're moving in, you can be my tutor and I'll just take the high school equivalency exam."

"It's not definite that we're moving in, Evan."

"I meant, if you do."

"I don't know if I can do that, Evan. I don't know if it's even legal," I said. "Doesn't the tutor have to be a licensed teacher?"

"Right," he snapped, looking down quickly. "It was a stupid idea. Forget it."

"I didn't say it was stupid, Evan."

He stopped talking. I could see how quickly he could be discouraged. Fooling around with him at lunch, meeting his challenges and quips with my own, had, strangely enough, gotten him to relax enough with me so that he was willing to talk with me and be with me privately. From the way his eyes traveled over my face, searching for sincerity, I could feel how difficult it was for him to place his trust in anyone. No wonder it was easier and far more comfortable for him to deal with people through a computer. There was so much less danger of being disappointed. If someone displeased you, you simply clicked the mouse and sent them into electronic oblivion.

"You wouldn't have the time for me, anyway," he finally said. "Once you started school here, you'd make lots of friends and wouldn't want to be tied down to some invalid, even the president of Invalids Anonymous."

"That's not true," I protested.

"Right. You just wouldn't be able to wait every day to rush home to help me with schoolwork. The truth is, you're probably the most popular girl in your school."

"The truth is, Evan, I don't have all that many friends at the school I'm at now," I revealed.

He looked up at me.

"Sure."

I stopped pushing his chair and walked around to the front so he would have to face me.

"For your information, Evan, I can count on the fingers of one hand the girls I care to talk to at school. Mommy, Daddy, and I have moved so many times, I never had a chance to make meaningful relationships. I can't even remember most of the other kids I knew. Their faces are like one big blur to me. It just so happens, our present address is the longest I can remember occupying, and it's not even a full two years!"

His self-pity dissolved as that look of interest and some trust seeped into his eyes again, warming them.

"I saw just how many places you've lived in. Why did you move so much?"

I looked off at the trees and folded my arms under my breasts.

"I used to think it was just because Daddy got bored easily or didn't care about important things as much as he should have, but after we learned about..."

"Me? The tragic accident of my birth?" he asked, the corners of his mouth turning down.

"I don't think of you as a tragic accident, Evan. Look, I expect I'll get to know you better, and maybe I won't like you. Maybe you're too bitter, so bitter that I won't be able to help," I said. "But from what I can see and what I've heard so far, you seem to be very intelligent. When I said I wasn't sure I could help you as your tutor, I was thinking to myself that you've already taught yourself so much, you probably know more than I do even though I'm two years older than you.

"Anyway," I continued, "yes, when we heard about you and your mother, both Mommy and I began to think that Daddy moved so much to avoid being pinned down by his added responsibilities. He was like that, I suppose," I said.

Evan's face softened further, making him look more like a little boy to me.

"I pretended I wasn't interested in him whenever Aunt Charlotte talked about him, but I would like to know more about him," he said. "I know I should hate him more than I could hate anyone, but I can't help wondering about him."

"I couldn't help loving him. I still love him. He was probably the most charming man I'll ever meet, but I can't deny being hurt and disappointed by what he's done, for Mommy as much as for myself. Maybe more than for myself," I added.

Evan stared at me and then, after a deep breath, said, "The reason I thought you wouldn't care to spend so much time with me is I thought you were so pretty, you surely had a string of boyfriends calling on you and would if you came here to live as well."

"Well, thank you, but I don't have a string of boyfriends."

"You won a beauty contest, didn't you?" he asked.

"No, I didn't win. I was first runner-up. Wait a minute," I said with my hands on my hips. "How did you know about that?"

"Aunt Charlotte told me. She had a detective."

"A detective? I thought she just had some attorneys doing some inquiries. A real detective?"

"Philip Marlowe himself," Evan joked. "I don't know, some retired policeman, I think. That must have been some beautiful girl to beat you."

"I'm not that beautiful, Evan."

"Can we promise each other that we won't lie to each other about the obvious at least, Rose? I'm crippled and you're pretty enough to be in the movies and that's that."

It was my turn to smile.

"She was related to the owner of the company," I revealed.

He laughed.

"I knew it. Don't you have at least one boyfriend, someone you like?"

"I'm seeing someone nice at the moment, yes," I admitted. "I'd like you to meet him."

He studied me for a moment and then looked down.

"No, you wouldn't," he said. "You're just being nice. You probably don't want anyone to know about me," he added, reverting to that bitterness. "There's no reason why you'd want anyone to know we're related."

"That's not true."

"My aunt promised your mother she'd keep it all secret. She told me."

"Well, it's embarrassing for her."

"And for you," he punched at me. "I'm just an embarrassment for everyone."

He spun his chair around and started pushing himself back toward the house.

I watched him for a moment and then shot forward and stopped him by putting my hands on his arms and leaning into him.

"Just a moment," I ordered.

"Let go. I got to get back to my room," he said. He glared at me, his eyes burning with anger and tears. He tried to thrust me aside, but I clung to his arms, weighing him and his wheelchair down so he couldn't move.

"No. You're going to stay here and listen. I'm not someone you can click off like you click people off on your computer."

"What?"

His face turned crimson with rage right down to his neck. I was sure his tantrums and explosions of anger always got him what he wanted, but my feet were planted firmly.

"You're not going anywhere until you promise to stop this. I certainly don't want to move in here and live with you if you're going to be like this all the time."

"Like what?"

"Like Mr. Self-pity."

I released my grip and stood up straight before him.

"Okay, we won't lie to each other about the obvious. You're right. This is not a lucky break for you and most people are not crippled and in a wheelchair, but you'd be surprised at how many people are crippled in other ways. For one thing, you're more intelligent than most people your age. I can see that immediately. You could probably do something wonderful with your life because of that and because of other talents you have that you don't even know about yourself.

"Most people who walk easily won't do something wonderful with their lives. I don't know if I'll do anything worth spit, but I'm not going to moan and groan about it. I'm going to make the best of what I have."

His eyebrows lifted.

"Really?"

"Yes, really. Daddy didn't do a good thing with your mother and you, I know, but he had a philosophy that helped him get by and often helped me face disappointments, too."

"And what exactly was this brilliant philosophy?" Evan asked, sitting back in his chair and folding his arms across his chest.

"He used to say there was no sense in worrying about things you have no control over." I smiled.

"What's so funny about that?" he asked.

"When I was a very little girl and something would bother me, he would always come into my room to stop me from crying or sulking."

"Terrific. Lucky you."

"One day," I continued, ignoring his sarcasm, "he brought a beautiful little wooden box in with him. It's this big," I said, holding my hands about a foot apart, "and it has that face of tragedy engraved on it on one side, and the face of happiness on the other...you know, what the Greeks used."

"You mean masks, not faces, and they originated with the Dionysian cult," he said.

I smiled at him.

"I bet you're a walking encyclopedia."

"Walking?"

"I mean..."

"I know," he said quickly. "Aunt Charlotte calls me Mr. Computer Head, so I had this T-shirt made up: Evan Dot Com. I ordered it over the Internet. It's where I do all my shopping now. But forget that. Tell me about the box," he said impatiently, like a child who didn't want to have a fairy tale end.

"Daddy said whenever something bad happened or something sad, I should write it down on a slip of paper and put it in the box and then turn the box so the happy face, the mask of comedy," I corrected, "is turned to me, and that would help me forget about it."

He nodded slowly. I expected some new sarcasm any moment, but he looked thoughtful.

"When you come here to live, if you actually do, be sure to bring the box along," he said. "I'll have lots to put in it," he added and wheeled himself forward. I watched him for a moment and then walked slowly after him, thinking that maybe we were more alike than either of us really knew or, more importantly, wanted to admit.

"Well, I see you two have been getting along like two sweet hummingbirds. That's wonderful," Charlotte cried as we returned to the patio.

"Yes, everything's going to be just peachy-keen

from now on, Aunt Charlotte," Evan said and continued to wheel himself past Mommy and Charlotte and into the house.

Mommy looked at me quizzically. I tilted my head a bit and smiled back at her with a slight shrug of my shoulders. She looked very anxious.

"Why don't I let you two talk a bit?" Charlotte said, looking from me to Mommy. "I have to make some social phone calls. I'm on so many committees these days."

She rose and went into the house, and I sat at the table watching the maid clear the food and dishes away.

"What do you think of all this, honey?" Mommy asked.

"I don't know, Mommy. It's certainly beautiful here."

"And look at what would be our rooms, and there are servants and no more money worries. She wants to take me shopping the day after tomorrow," Mommy continued excitedly. "She says I must have what she calls 'decent clothes' to wear because she does a great deal of socializing and I must be part of all that now. I must say, my head is whirling. Parties, dinners, dances, trips to Atlanta to the theater, and she will pay for everything. Such generosity."

"Did she indicate any more specifically what she expects from you, Mommy?" I asked suspiciously.

Mommy shook her head.

"Just to be here, to help create a feeling of family, to help her cope, I suppose. It doesn't sound very difficult. She's looking for a companion, someone her own age, I think."

"Why would a woman with all this need to draft a companion, Mommy?"

"I don't know all the answers, Rose, but should we look a gift horse in the mouth?" she asked.

"I guess not."

"Did you get along with Evan?"

"He's a very sensitive and angry person," I said.

"Who needs someone like you," Mommy insisted. I could see Charlotte had done a wonderful sales job, not that she needed all that many different ways to persuade. The house, the grounds, all of it was enough for anyone to give up her life without a second thought.

"Maybe," I said cautiously.

"So shall we say yes, Rose?" Mommy asked me.

I took a deep breath. We were going to move again. Even Daddy's death didn't stop that now. Mommy looked so excited about it, so enthusiastic. How could I even think of putting up any obstacles at this terrible time in her life?

I nodded.

"Okay, Mommy," I said. "Let's move in."

She clapped her hands and then reached out to hug me.

Charlotte must have been watching us from inside that patio door because she was out just as we embraced.

"Does that mean yes?" she asked Mommy.

"It does," Mommy said.

Charlotte smiled.

"Welcome then, you two. My home is now yours as

well." She turned to me and added, "Evan will be so pleased. Come upstairs, Monica. I must show you this new outfit I bought at Saks last week. I think we're almost the same size," she added.

"Her closet is like a department store. She has clothing with the tags still hanging off," Mommy whispered, and then she leaped to her feet and started toward her. Just before she entered the house she looked back at me and beamed a smile as she raised her arms.

"We're due for a little luck," she called back to me and disappeared.

I looked out over the grounds toward the shadows in the forest.

A little luck, yes, but is it good luck or bad? I wondered.

Time keeps all the secrets buried under weeks and days, hours and minutes, and we poor unfortunate souls have to pluck them away second by second, searching for our discoveries, our great moments of pleasure and happiness, and our great moments of terrible disappointments and sadness, I thought.

How soon would we know what secrets awaited us here? I felt confident there would be more than one.

Mommy was so eager to go home and start our packing, she was downstairs and ready to leave as soon as possible. Charlotte offered to hire people to help, but Mommy explained that we had so little of real value to bring with us, it wasn't necessary.

"We'll donate our pathetic furniture to the Salvation

Army," she told Charlotte. "Not a piece of it would belong here anyway."

Pathetic? I thought. Once it was special to us; once we were happy about the house we had rented and the furnishing we were able to manage. Now, that was all to be discarded like so many of our recent memories. I knew if Mommy could, she would wipe her mind clear like some magic slate. She would be like Daddy was and think, *Forget the past. Concentrate only on the here and now.* How sad it was that we had very little to cling to, to bring with us.

Even our photo albums, full of pictures from so many different places, so many homes, looked more like a travelogue than a family history.

"I'm happy about that," Charlotte told Mommy and then looked at me as well to add, "You're both starting a new life, Rose. Let everything be fresh. We're going to take you shopping for new clothes, too, and new shoes to match. Don't even bring an old toothbrush. I have new ones in your bathroom cabinets."

Mommy laughed and the two of them walked out arm in arm as if they were already old, dear friends.

"I'll say good-bye to Evan," I shouted after them.

"Oh, yes, do that, and be sure to tell him you'll be back tomorrow."

"Tomorrow, but that's so quick, Mommy. I have school and I have to..."

"Charlotte has arranged it all, Rose. You're enrolled in the school here already, remember? The administration is getting your transcripts in the morning."

"How did..." I didn't finish the question. Mommy had already turned away. I finished it in my thoughts, however. *How did she know we would accept and come here for sure?*

It put a cold but electric feeling through my veins and made my heart thump for a few moments. Were we so desperate and forlorn that anyone could come along and hold our destinies in the wind like kites and watch us be blown from one place to another? I could feel it. Whatever little control we had of ourselves was drifting away.

Daddy had done a great deal more than he had ever dreamed when he had his love affair with Angelica and a child with her, I thought.

Evan's door was open this time, but he was back where I had found him previously, at his computer.

"Hi," I said. He wasn't wearing earphones. "I guess it's happening. We're actually moving in tomorrow," I said. He kept working as if he hadn't heard me. "Did you hear what I said, Evan?"

"Yes, but I knew that was going to happen," he replied, still working the keyboard and looking at the monitor.

"How did..."

"Wait. There," he said and turned. I heard the printer going. "It's coming out." He nodded at the printer, which was on the table to his right. I walked in and waited by it, watching as the picture began emerging. I felt the heat building in my neck and face as it was forming. Finally, it was done, and I picked it up.

It was a picture of Daddy, me, Evan, Mommy, and his mother Angelica, all together.

"How did you do this?"

"It's not hard," he said. "I had pictures of everyone and scanned them in together to make that. There it is, the big happy family."

It gave me the chills.

"Where did you get this picture of Daddy?"

"Aunt Charlotte found it in my mother's things. I got your picture and your mother's from the file Aunt Charlotte's detective made.

"I was going to put Aunt Charlotte in there, too, sort of in the background like some puppeteer or something. What do you think? Should I?"

I stared at him.

He smiled.

"Come here, watch this," he said, and began working again. He brought up a picture of Charlotte, cut off her head and pasted on the body of a small gorilla. I laughed and then he put her head on the body of a naked, buxom woman.

"Evan!"

"It's magic. I can turn anyone into anything. Look what I did for you," he said and clicked something that was already completed.

It came up on the screen. He had taken the photo of Sheila Stone from the newspaper story of the Miss Lewisville Foundry Beauty Contest and substituted me with the crown on my head.

"See how easy it is to right the wrongs?"

I laughed, and he clicked again and brought up a picture of himself riding a horse, and then one with him running in an Olympic race.

"I wish that was real, Evan," I said softly.

He smiled at me.

"It is real. This is make-believe," he said, indicating his wheelchair.

Daddy would agree, I thought. *Daddy would love this.*

"You've got your own magic box," I said softly, gazing at his computer monitor.

"Exactly," he said, smiling, and I wondered if I really would help him or harm him by doing what Charlotte had hoped I would do: bring him out of this room and away from his own world.

6

A New Life

Mommy attacked our home with a vengeance. It was as if she was getting back at all the bad luck and hard times she had ever suffered after marrying Daddy. Anything that in the slightest way provided a painful or unpleasant memory was eagerly dropped into the garbage cans, no matter what its monetary value. She did the same with things I had thought were important reminders of her relationship with Daddy.

I was really surprised at how she sifted through her wardrobe, selecting so many dresses, blouses, pants, and even shoes to give away. None of it was worn-out or faded. When I questioned her, she turned to me and said, "You heard Charlotte. What point would there be in bringing these clothes to that house? They're so out of style, she wouldn't want me to wear them anyway. And besides," she added like a little girl just before

Christmas, "she's buying me a whole new wardrobe. You heard her."

"Maybe she was just exaggerating, Mommy."

She thought a moment and then shook her head, first slowly and then vigorously as she convinced herself more and more.

"No, no, Rose, she wants us there too much and she doesn't want us to be unhappy and leave. No. For the first time, what little old me wants is going to be important."

She then advised me to do the same thing: scrutinize my clothing and pack in boxes whatever was too old or out of style.

"You'll give it away along with all my stuff," she told me, but I didn't listen.

Something inside told me to beware of being too beholden to Charlotte Alden Curtis. Maybe it was the manner in which Evan spoke of her and showed what he really thought of her. His sarcastic remarks about her seemed sharper to me than they were about anyone or anything else, and when he looked at her, he always seemed to narrow his eyes with suspicion and distrust. I realized of course that it could just be his way. He had first looked at me in a similar fashion. Still, I wasn't as optimistic about the move as Mommy was. In the back of my mind, I saw it as just another pit stop on the way to some other destination Fate had already determined for us.

While I was packing, Barry called, and it occurred to me how strange and curious my sudden departure from our school would seem to all the other students. Paula would surely use it as confirmation of her theories and justification for her rumors. *But what difference does all that make to me now anyway?* I thought. *I will be gone from here forever.*

Barry was stunned at the suddenness of our moving. I explained how it was an opportunity for us that we couldn't afford to pass up and how it provided a solution to our financial dilemma. Mommy and I had concocted a cover story for our instant move, a story she was using with the landlord as well. According to Mommy, Mrs. Curtis was an old friend of my daddy's family and needed someone to help her with the care of her invalid nephew since the unfortunate death of his mother. It was a fiction based on some truth, which made Mommy more comfortable about our lies.

"Oh, sure," Barry said. "I can understand all that. Actually, you're not that far away anyhow. Can I come out to take you to dinner Saturday?"

"I'd like that," I said and promised to call and give him my own phone number as soon as it had been established.

I was very happy that he wouldn't give up on me so easily. We talked a little longer. He asked questions about Evan and Charlotte, but I was able to simply say I didn't know enough about it all yet. It bothered me to have to throw up a wall of deceit between us. I was more comfortable and at ease with Barry than I had been with any other boy and I liked him very much.

Daddy's exploits had shown me what deception

could do to a relationship. It made every word uttered and every kiss given seem like just so much smoke. If someone didn't know himself where his heart belonged, how could you ever trust his promises or his claims of love? How similar had Daddy's words of love with Angelica been to the words of love he pressed with his lips into Mommy's ear? Did all men practice one set of romantic and cherished utterances on every woman they met and wanted? Without trust there could be no love, I decided, and understood why Evan had so dark a vision for himself. He surely believed he would be without love his whole life.

Could I change that? Did I want even to try? Was I the right person for the task anyway? At the moment, still recovering from what Daddy had done to us, I was one of those crippled people I had described to Evan. How could I convince him to open his heart to anyone? How could I promise him rainbows? I was still under the dark clouds myself.

It was very difficult falling asleep for the last time in this house. Butterflies circled themselves in my stomach every time I thought about what we were committing ourselves to do. To me it looked like Charlotte Alden Curtis was using us, as if we were some sort of Band-Aid to cover the rips and tears in the fabric of her own tattered family life. It was surely like asking the blind to lead the blind, I thought. Mommy wasn't really strong enough to be anyone's crutch. She had trouble standing on her own two feet.

When I did finally fall asleep, I tossed and turned so

much, I found the blanket wrapped so tightly around my legs in the morning it was as if I was trying to tie myself down to keep myself from rising and going through with the move.

Mommy was up at the blink of sunlight through the veil of clouds that were daubed over the pale blue morning sky. I heard her bustling about, making final checks of drawers and closets and then marching up and down the hallway and stairs, deliberately making more noise than usual so I would get up and join her. Finally, she called to me.

"Don't forget Charlotte is sending the car at ten, Rose. We want to be ready!"

Ready? Would we ever be ready for this? I wondered, but rose, showered, and dressed in jeans and one of Daddy's old flannel shirts he had given me months ago.

"Why didn't you throw out that shirt?" Mommy asked the moment she set eyes on me. "You don't want to go to a house like that wearing some old, smelly shirt, Rose."

"It's not smelly, Mommy, and I don't expect we'll have to dress up every day, all day, just because it's a mansion."

"Well, I've decided to do something about myself," Mommy explained as she poured her coffee and sat at the table. "I'm going to get rid of this haggard, old-lady look, do what Charlotte suggested and get an up-to-date hairstyle, take more care with my makeup, and dress nicely all the time. I want to look like I belong in that house.

"She's really not any more attractive than I am, is she?"

"No, she's not, Mommy."

"But she looks like she is because of the way she dresses and how she takes care of herself. Your father had me thinking those things didn't matter much. He was happy keeping me locked up in this house. That's why he was never very enthusiastic about any jobs I had.

"Now," she added, her lips tightening, "we know why."

Despite all Daddy had done, I couldn't get myself to harden my heart against him. He was dead and gone, but his smile lingered on my eyes and his laughter still echoed in my ears. He must have loved us. He must have, I told myself.

Charlotte's chauffeur Ames helped us load the car. Mommy had arranged for the landlord to take possession of most of the good furniture and even the kitchenware in lieu of our rental obligations. We were really leaving the house with as little as possible, which was just what Mommy, and apparently Charlotte Alden Curtis, wanted. I had the most and Mommy didn't stop complaining about it.

When we arrived at the Curtis mansion, Ames and Nancy Sue brought in most of our things and put away what belonged in each of our rooms. Nancy Sue began to hang up Mommy's clothes first and then came in to do mine. Mommy was so excited and pleased about that.

"I never had a maid, even when I lived with my parents," she told me in a loud whisper. "Imagine having someone care for your clothes and clean your bathroom, making sure you have all that you require. I can get used to this fast. I surely can," she declared.

She did look like a little girl who had been brought to a toy store and told she could have whatever she wanted.

"I made your hair appointment," I heard Charlotte tell her in the hallway soon afterward. "Two o'clock."

"Today!" Mommy exclaimed.

"Why wait?" Charlotte replied, and Mommy squealed with delight.

I came out just as Charlotte was telling her where they were going to go to lunch first.

"I think you should wear my Donna Karan suit. Come try it on," she urged.

Mommy flashed a bright smile at me and raised her eyebrows.

"Are you settling in nicely?" Charlotte asked me.

"Yes," I said.

"Whatever you need, just tell Nancy Sue. Tomorrow morning, Ames will drive you to school. Everything is all set there. It will be like you've always attended."

"I doubt that," I said. "I've been a new student in enough schools to tell you it's never easy."

"This time it will be," Charlotte assured me. "I'm a rather big contributor to the fund."

Fund? What fund? I wondered.

"Isn't that wonderful?" Mommy pressed on.

"We'll see," I said cautiously.

"Relax, enjoy the house today, and get to know

Evan better," Charlotte said. "At the moment his tutor is with him, but she leaves in less than an hour. Oh, your phone is already connected."

"Isn't that wonderful?" Mommy asked me. I had to admit, it did overwhelm me.

"Come along, Monica. We've got a lot to do," Charlotte insisted before I could utter another word.

"I'm right behind you," Mommy cried, and the two of them went off.

I stood there for a moment, listening to them giggling like teenage girls. Was I wrong in being so hesitant and doubtful? A part of me was happy for the way in which Charlotte Alden Curtis had wiped the gray stains of depression off Mommy's eyes and replaced them with a childlike glee, but a part of me still remained very nervous. I was like someone waiting for that famous second shoe to drop. I didn't know where or how it would drop, but it would. I was sure.

Maybe I was just envious, just wishing I could be like that, too.

I decided I would take Charlotte's advice and relax and enjoy the house. I took more time in the library, impressed with all the books, the leather-bound editions of the classics and the collections of old magazines. The family room had a wide-screen television set and a state-of-the-art sound system, and a beautiful dark hickory-wood pool table.

In the kitchen Nancy Sue was preparing lunch for me and for Evan. Instead of asking me what I liked, she was going to set out a variety of luncheon meats, breads, and cheeses. It seemed like wasted effort and even wasted food, but when I commented about it, she told me it was what Mrs. Curtis ordered. From the tone of Nancy Sue's voice, I understood that when Charlotte spoke, it was gospel.

The pale blue sky had become more vibrantly blue with every passing hour, and the thin veil of clouds had drifted west. We were having another one of those unusually warm days for this time of the year. I strolled along the same path I had followed with Evan the day before until, this time, I reached an oak tree. I was drawn to the trunk when I spotted what looked like carving. It turned out to be Evan's initials and what I guessed were his mother's initials. I really hadn't thought much about his relationship with his mother and how deeply he must have suffered her loss. He had said so little about her yesterday. Were they close? How did she treat him? What had she told him about Daddy? I probably had as many questions for him as he had for me.

When I turned to start back to the house, I saw him out on the patio watching me.

"I've got to get fresh air as soon as my tutor leaves," he explained when I approached. "I actually tried spraying some of my mother's old perfume around the room before she comes, but it doesn't seem powerful enough to overcome the stink."

I laughed.

"Why don't you just tell her?"

"So she goes complaining about me to my aunt Charlotte? No thanks. I'm tired of hearing how ungrateful I can be. I see you were looking at my tree. It was planted just about the time I was born."

"Then those are definitely your initials?"

"And my mother's. She used to bring me out there for a picnic. She'd set out a blanket and play the radio or her CDs and we'd look at the clouds and describe what they suggested to us. Often, we both fell asleep. Aunt Charlotte said we brought ants back into the house in our clothing or in the blanket."

"What would your mother say to that?"

"Nothing really. She had a way of just looking at her and smiling a smile that said, 'Don't be silly, Charlotte.' It was enough to shut her up."

"I imagine you miss her a great deal."

He stared at me a moment, his eyes glassing over.

"As much as you miss our daddy, if not more," he finally said. "Did you bring the magic box?"

"Yes," I replied, smiling.

"Good. Put this in it for me," he said and held out his hand with a slip of paper between his thumb and forefinger. I took it.

"What is it?"

"A disappointment," he replied.

"Can I look?"

"You probably would anyway."

"I would not. It's your personal disappointment. I'm not the sort of person who..."

"Okay, okay. Look already and spare me the speeches."

I unfolded it and read the word, *Arlene.*

"Arlene? That's your disappointment?"

He shrugged.

"She was my cyber girlfriend until late yesterday, when she decided to break up and go into a private chat room with someone else."

I shook my head, a confused smile on my face.

"It's how I go out on a date," he explained. "We talk to each other in a private chat room. She and I got along really well and had some good times. I guess I wasn't sexy enough."

"Sexy enough? How can you be sexy on the computer?"

He smiled.

"You'll see. One of these days."

"Lunch," Nancy Sue announced from the doorway.

"Good. Now that I drove Mrs. Skulnik out of my nose, I'm hungry," he said and started to wheel himself into the house.

I hurried to catch up, wondering what he was talking about when he talked about cyber dates.

He asked me so many questions at lunch, I was barely able to chew my food and swallow. Mostly, he wanted to know what my school experiences were like. When I began in a new school, did I always gravitate toward a certain clique of friends? What kind of people did I like?

And what about my classes? Was there a great deal of flirting always going on behind the teacher's back? How many school dances had I attended? Did I have a boyfriend I regretted losing so much that I was actually in physical pain? Was I ever on a team or a cheerleader or in a play and what was that like? On and on it went, making me feel he was truly like someone who had just arrived from another planet.

"I can't imagine really learning in such a setting," he finally said after hearing some of my school experiences. "There's so much to draw away your attention. Did you ever go to an all girls' school?" he asked quickly. "Without members of the opposite sex present, it might be easier. Well?"

He was so impatient for my responses, he couldn't wait for me to start to talk.

"No, Evan."

"I can't imagine not being related to you and being in a class with you," he suddenly said, but he said it like a scientist evaluating data. "I'd be looking at you all the time and never concentrating."

I smiled, even though he had made it sound like cold analysis.

"You're going to give me a big head, Evan. There were always prettier girls in my classes."

"I doubt that. I've never been in school like you, but I've seen plenty of girls."

"Oh?"

"There's this personal dating service on the Internet where the girls put up pictures of themselves and describe themselves. Then boys send them their pictures and descriptions and they communicate for a while to see if it might work into anything. I've done it plenty of times. Of course, I substitute pictures so they never see me like this," he said, indicating the wheelchair.

"What's to keep anyone from doing the same?"

"Nothing, if that's all they want to do. But if they actually want to meet someday, they better show the truth, don't you think?"

I nodded.

"I have no illusions about it. The chat is as far as I'll be able to go."

"You never wanted to meet this Arlene?"

"No," he said quickly. "Maybe she dumped me because she found out the truth about me. Besides, I'm not talking about her anymore, remember. She's going into your magic box," he reminded me.

I laughed and nodded.

"Right."

"What about that boy you're seeing? Does he know you've actually moved?"

"Yes, and he's coming to take me to dinner on Saturday. You'll meet him. His name is Barry Burton."

"Great alliteration."

"Pardon?"

"You know, B and B? The repetition of consonants?"

"Oh. I bet you have one of those very high IQs, don't you?"

"Off the charts," he said smugly.

"What do you want to do, to be, Evan?"

He thought a moment.

"I guess I'll become a brain surgeon. What they'll do is make a platform by the operating table and I'll wheel up on it and lean over the patient's head."

I stared at him coldly.

"I don't know," he said in a softer tone. "I like to write. I've been working on a play."

"Really? Can I read it?"

"No," he said quickly.

"Why not?"

"It's nowhere near ready and it's not any good. It's just a dumb idea."

"Why don't you let me be the judge of that?"

"Oh? And you are a critic?"

"No, but I've been in plays, as I told you, and I would be honest."

He stared a moment and then he shrugged.

"Maybe I'll show it to you later."

"I'd like that," I said.

After lunch we went outside and I got him to talk a little more about his mother. I listened, practically holding my breath for fear he would stop.

"Sometimes—often, I should say—I felt she was more like the child and I was more like the parent. She was so trusting and always saw the best in everyone, even Aunt Charlotte. She had a beautiful laugh, musical, and she sang to me all the time. 'I'll be your legs, Evan,' she told me. 'Forever and ever if need be, so don't feel sorry for yourself.'

"She never thought she would die before me, I know. She thought I was so fragile I would surely pass away one day, just evaporate or something, and she would be at my side.

"When I was young, she was overprotective, afraid I would catch every little germ. The doctors kept assuring her that aside from my, what did you call it, unfortunate situation? Aside from that, I was relatively as healthy as any other person my age. Of course, I don't have the athletic abilities. I tried building up my arms and my chest, but she was always worried I was doing too much and after a while I stopped doing that.

"She liked it when I read to her. We read a lot of poetry together and we even read plays together and performed out there by the tree. She did a great Juliet, but I was a lousy Romeo.

"Aunt Charlotte complained, telling her she was doting on me too much and sacrificing herself too much. She told her she should be out socializing with young men, finding someone. She could have easily, I suppose. She was beautiful, as beautiful as you," he added.

"She looks beautiful in every picture I've seen of her," I said softly.

"Yeah. Aunt Charlotte was always after her to get out, mix with people. I think she was hoping my mother would find a man, marry, and take me away so she wouldn't have to deal with all this. Poor Aunt Charlotte got stuck with me. She would send her out to meet some blind date she had arranged through one of her society friends sometimes. She would harp on it and badger her so much, my mother would finally agree.

"What kind of a date was it where she had to go meet the guy somewhere anyway, huh?" he demanded, his eyes beginning to burn with hot tears. "Why couldn't he just come here and pick her up? Don't people go out on dates like that anymore?" he asked me. "Maybe Aunt Charlotte was afraid they would see me and be frightened off.

"It was the same sort of thing the night she was killed," he said. "Why did she have to go out that night?"

He wiped a fugitive tear from his cheek quickly.

"I'll write it on a piece of paper for the magic box," he said, and took a deep breath. "But I don't think there's enough magic even in that box."

He smiled.

"I keep her alive in my own magic box, but she's alive in so many ways. See those rose bushes over there?"

I looked and nodded.

"She planted those bushes. They're her roses and when they come up, they remind me of her. I think of them as waiting for her to prune them, nurture them. Sometimes, I see a shadow move or hear a footstep in the hallway and expect her to come walking into my room, her smile beaming at me, her voice light and full of laughter.

"You think of me as full of self-pity, but it was difficult to be that way with my mother. She just refused to let gray skies over our heads. If anything made us sad even for an instant, we were to close our eyes and think of blue. 'There!' she would cry, 'It's beautiful now. Isn't it, Evan?'

"I felt obligated to make her happy and agree. You know what I mean?"

"Yes," I said. "Daddy was like that."

"Mm. Maybe that's what drew them together. I wonder what *their* first date was like," hc thought aloud and then looked down at his hands in his lap, lowering his head like some flag of defeat.

"I'd like to see how someone goes on a date over the Internet," I said to help move him from his terrible sorrow.

He raised his eyes to me quickly.

"Really?"

"I don't know as much as other people my age do about computers. I started the course this year, but I've got a lot to learn yet."

"It's easy," he said. "Aunt Charlotte thinks it's rocket science, but she doesn't even know how to work the microwave oven. She's never had to do much for herself. I'll show you most of it in a few hours," he promised, permitting excitement to enter his voice.

"I'd like that, Evan. Thanks."

He smiled coyly.

"What?" I asked.

"I'll show you one of my computer dates, but you've got to share your date, too. You've got to tell me about it, okay?"

"Sure," I said.

It seemed innocent enough.

But I didn't know what he meant, how much he really wanted from me. Despite all his electronic relationships and connections, he was really very lonely. It showed in his shadowed eyes.

And then I thought, maybe Charlotte wasn't so wrong. Maybe she expected I would fill in some of the empty places that Evan's mother once occupied for him. It wasn't a bad thing to want for him, I thought. Perhaps she did care about him and feel terribly sorry for him. Who could blame her for bringing us into her home if that was truly the reason? It made me feel bad for doubting her or distrusting her.

But then I thought again about the lesson in the allegory of Plato's Cave: Things are not always what they seem to be. Wait, wait for the last bit of darkness and shadow to fall victim to the light, and then look again, think again, feel again.

Then you will know what is true and what is not.

7

Heart of the Angel

I had no idea how much time I had spent in Evan's room watching him work his computer and learning about it. I couldn't help but be fascinated by the exchanges going on between the boys and girls he and I watched in the so-called dating room.

"I used to date this girl, too," he told me. "Her screen name is Dreamluv. She didn't change her dating room password so I can eavesdrop."

He looked at me and smiled.

"I think she wants me to listen in. It's her way of teasing me. She thinks it bothers me, I guess. I blew her off two days ago," he said.

"How old is she?"

"She says she's seventeen, but from her vocabulary and responses, I'd say she's more like twelve, wouldn't you?"

"I can't believe this," I remarked when I saw that the conversation between Dreamluv and her supposed new boyfriend Spunky was rapidly becoming raunchy and quite vulgar. They began to tell each other things to do to themselves and then report the results.

"Disgusting!" I cried, and Evan clicked them off instantly.

"Now you've seen cyber sex," he remarked with a casual shrug.

"I don't want to see it. It makes me sick to my stomach."

"For most of these people," he said, nearly in a whisper so that I had to struggle to hear him, "it's all they have. They're either too shy or they think they're too ugly to meet people face to face. Some of them are in my Invalids Anonymous organization. I'm sorry if it upset you."

Before I could respond, I heard Mommy's and Charlotte's voices echoing down the hallway. The sounds of their laughter and their shoes clicking over the tile floors brought my eyes to the clock.

"They're back! Look what time it is. We've been here for hours, Evan."

He shrugged.

"Sometimes I'm here all day. I even have lunch brought to me, and occasionally dinner."

"I'd better see what Mommy's done. Thanks for showing your computer to me."

I went out to greet Mommy and see what her hair was like now and stopped dead when I saw. She had a hairdo that was practically a carbon copy of Charlotte's. She was wearing Charlotte's designer outfit and her makeup was different too: a far brighter shade of lipstick, and more vivid rouge and eyeliner. She had an armful of boxes, and there were more boxes at her feet.

"Oh, Rose, come quickly and help me with some of this," she cried.

"What is all that and what have you done to your hair, Mommy?"

"Don't you like it?" she asked, turning to model her coiffure.

"I took her to my personal beautician," Charlotte said, "who treated her with lots of tender loving care."

She stood off to the side gloating at her new creation like a Doctor Frankenstein.

"Well?" Mommy asked, waiting for my response.

"We brought your mother into the twenty-first century," Charlotte bragged.

"It's not you, Mommy," I said, and Mommy's smile wilted quickly. "You're wearing too much makeup, too," I complained. "It's gross."

Charlotte laughed.

"Really, dear, your mother was made up by a cosmetic expert at the department store."

"I don't care. It's too much for her," I insisted. "You look... cheap," I said.

"Oh, my," Charlotte said, bringing her hand to the base of her throat.

"That's enough, Rose," Mommy snapped at me. "Help me with these packages. We're taking it all up to my room."

I gathered what I could.

"Where's Evan?" Charlotte asked.

"At his computer," I said.

"Really?" She grimaced like someone who had bitten into a rotten hard-boiled egg. "I was hoping you might draw him away from all that," Charlotte said and shifted her eyes quickly toward Mommy, whose eyes turned nervous with fear that I had somehow let her down.

"We did spend almost an hour and a half outside talking," I said.

"Good. A little more every day and maybe you'll get him to become social and normal."

"He is normal," I insisted. "He's just in a great deal of pain."

"Not according to his doctors and nurses," Charlotte bounced back at me.

"I'm not talking about that kind of pain. I'm talking about the pain in his heart," I said.

"Oh, well, perhaps you can help him forget that," she continued. "It's why I wanted y'all here, you know," she added, the timbre in her voice colder, more formal.

"Of course she will," Mommy quickly said. "Won't you, Rose?"

"I don't know, Mommy," I said honestly.

"Well, I do," Charlotte said. "You will. We will lift the gloom and doom out of this house and bring it back to its glorious days when the halls were filled with laughter, the rooms were stuffed with wonderful, good-looking people and music and the clinking of champagne glasses, or we will die trying, won't we, Monica?"

Mommy smiled and laughed.

"Yes, Charlotte, oh, yes."

"We met some nice people at lunch, didn't we?"

"Yes," Mommy said. "We did."

"Especially that Grover Fleming," Charlotte said, her voice full of teasing. "He nearly wore lines in your face with the intensity of his looks. I've never seen him so infatuated with anyone. And he's a catch, worth *millions!*" she emphasized.

"He was very nice," Mommy admitted. Her eyes looked as dream filled as a teenager's.

"And don't forget we've been invited to dinner in Atlanta this weekend," Charlotte continued.

"Dinner?" I asked. "But how... who?"

"Friends of Charlotte's," Mommy said.

"Grover will be there," Charlotte added.

"I'll tell you all about it later," Mommy said. "Let's take all this up now, please," she insisted and started up the stairway.

I glanced back at Charlotte. Her look of cold satisfaction put a stick of ice on the back of my neck.

As soon as we entered Mommy's room, she began to unpack her things to show me one outfit after another, matching shoes, new blouses, belts, even some expensive-looking costume jewelry.

"The saleswoman said I looked ten years younger

in this," she told me when she held up a burgundy pantsuit.

"When I looked at the price, I nearly fainted, but Charlotte didn't blink an eyelash. Take a guess at how much she spent on me today. Go on. Take a guess."

"I don't care, Mommy. This is...sick."

"Sick? Why?"

"Why would she do all this for you and spend so much money on you?"

"We've been all through that, Rose," Mommy said, dropping the outfit onto her bed and reaching for hangers. "It's a trade-off. I don't feel a bit guilty or strange about any of it either. We'll earn our keep here, I'm sure. You've already started becoming friends with Evan and helping him, haven't you?"

"I'm not doing it to earn my keep, Mommy. He is my half-brother, isn't he?"

"Charlotte's told me so much about him, how introverted he really is and how much it troubles her," she continued as if I had not spoken. "You know he's never gone to a movie? He doesn't want to go for rides or go into the city. She has to pull teeth to get him to get new clothes and shoes. He doesn't care what he wears, and look at his hair! She's considered having him drugged and then having a stylist sneak in and do him one night."

"Brilliant. That's sure to bring him out," I said and plopped into the French Provincial chair in her sitting area.

Mommy paid little or no attention to me. Her eyes were fixed on each outfit as she hung it up and described how she had looked in it when she had put it on in the store.

"The other salespeople came around to remark how nicely everything fit me," she continued. "I had my own little fan club for part of the afternoon, just the way you did that day I bought you your outfits for the beauty contest, remember?"

"They do that only to get you to buy things, Mommy," I said.

"Now, Rose, they knew we were going to buy things. They didn't have to do anything. Charlotte's well-known in these stores. The way they cater to her, jump and drop everything they're doing when she appears...it took my breath away to see such devotion."

"It's not devotion. It's servitude. They're beholden to her for what she spends there."

"It's the same thing in the end, isn't it, Rose? Who would you rather be, the salesgirl or Charlotte?"

"Never Charlotte," I insisted.

Mommy laughed at me as if I was saying the silliest things. I found myself getting more and more infuriated. I could see from the way she paused to gaze at herself in her vanity mirror every other minute that she was infatuated with her new look.

"Why did you let them cut your hair like that, Mommy?"

"When did I ever have the money or the chance to be in style, Rose? Why, I could see the difference the moment we walked out of that salon. Men on the street were pausing to look my way. Even men in automobiles turned toward us. It's been a long time since I turned a man's eyes to me like that. I've been living in a cocoon your father wove around me all these years. Who had time or the inclination to be beautiful before this, or even care?

"This," she said, pausing and holding one of her new dresses against her bosom as she gazed about the room, "is like a miracle. To get a second chance at life at my age."

"You're not that old, Mommy."

"You're as old as you feel," she countered, "and when I was living back in that...that life, I felt old. Suddenly, it's as if I have sipped from the fountain of youth."

She closed her eyes and then she opened them on me.

"You'll see. You'll begin to enjoy all this, too. Wait until you attend that school tomorrow and make friends with boys and girls from well-established families. You won't complain about the gossip and the jealousies."

"That's ridiculous, Mommy," I said, scrunching my face in amazement. "There's probably twice as much."

"Nonsense. When you have all this, you don't feel threatened and you don't have to tear someone else down to make yourself feel good. Why, they'll all appreciate you more, Rose. You'll see."

She continued putting her new things away. She seemed like some stranger to me, saying things, having ideas I had never heard from her lips before. I didn't know whether to be more frightened or angry.

"What's this dinner you're going to this weekend?"

"A dinner at one of the fanciest hotels in Atlanta where there's an orchestra playing while you eat. See why I needed better clothing?"

"Barry's coming to take me out to dinner Saturday," I said.

She stopped putting away her clothes and turned to me.

"Really, dear, don't you think you should shed the past? You'll meet far nicer and finer boys tomorrow, and I'm sure before the week's out, you'll be asked on a date. You don't want to have to refuse someone from here because you've failed to cut the ties to that other place, now do you?"

Tears came to my eyes, tears of definite anger and disappointment. I took a deep breath and stood.

"Yes, I do," I said. "I don't measure people by their bank accounts, and when I meet someone as nice as Barry I don't turn him away in hopes that I'll meet someone who lives in a mansion, Mommy."

"You'll learn," she said, shaking her head and darkening her eyes with pity. "I was hoping our lives, my mistakes would have been enough to drive it home by now, but hopefully, you'll learn."

"That's a lesson I'd rather skip, Mommy. You used to say that real love is true wealth."

"That's something poor people tell themselves to make themselves feel better, Rose. Love," she said, shaking her head. "It's a soap bubble, full of rainbow colors, but as soon as you touch it, it pops and you have nothing but some illusion to remember.

"I'd rather remember all this," she said, nodding at the walls as if they were made of gold. "You'll see."

She thought a moment and then she laughed.

"Did I show you the necklace and earrings? They're made of that material that resembles diamonds. You can't tell the difference. It's called Diamond Air, Cubic Zirconia."

"Really, Mommy," I said. "Someone who has the wealth and background you're raving about would surely be smart enough to know the difference," I said.

She considered what I said and then shrugged.

"Well then, he'll decide to buy me the real thing, won't he?"

She laughed and turned back to her closet. I sat there a moment staring at her and then got up and left. She didn't even know I had.

I wasn't comfortable being driven to school by a chauffeur, but Charlotte insisted and Mommy was like her cheering section, urging me to agree to each and every suggestion concerning me that Charlotte made. At breakfast, she even had the audacity to suggest I cut my hair more like theirs, too.

"Then we'll all look alike," I said.

"What of it?" Charlotte asked, her eyes blinking with innocence.

"One size doesn't fit all when it comes to things like that. I'm me. You're you. Mommy's..."

"Mommy," Charlotte said. She looked at her and Mommy turned away. There was a time, only hours ago, it seemed, when that would have brought pride to her eyes, not shame and embarrassment. "Can't you call her Monica?"

"What? She's my mother. Why do I have to call her Monica?" I asked.

"Calling her Mommy just makes her sound... older," she insisted. "At least do it in front of any guests we have," she requested.

Again, I looked at Mommy to see if she would disagree, but she was silent and threw me a small smile.

"Is that what you would like me to do, Mommy?"

"I don't see why it's such a world-shattering thing," Charlotte pursued.

"You don't have a daughter or a son," I said sharply. "You're not a mother."

"Rose," Mommy chastised, shifting her gaze at Charlotte.

"That's all right, Monica," Charlotte said in her sweet Southern voice. "Rose happens to be correct."

She turned back to me, her eyes narrowing.

"No, I'm not a mother, dear." She laughed a cold, mechanical laugh. "But after seeing what most mothers, and fathers, I should add, put up with these days, I can't say I feel deprived and disappointed. Modern children are so unappreciative. They think everything is coming to them just because they were brought into this world. They almost want to punish their parents for having the nerve to conceive them. You know what I'm talking about, don't you, Monica? We were discussing it yesterday in the car after we saw that poor woman being nagged to death by her spoiled daughter at Tiffany's."

"Yes," Mommy said quickly.

I turned to her sharply.

"Fine," I said. "From now on, I'll call you Monica, Monica. I'd better get on my way. I don't want to be late for my first day in my new, wonderful school. Am I dressed stylishly enough?"

"Oh, don't worry about that," Charlotte said with a small laugh that brought curiosity to my facc.

"Go on, dear," Mommy said. "I'm sure you have a lot to do."

"Of course she does," Charlotte said.

I marched out of the dining room and almost fell over Evan who was sitting back in his wheelchair just outside the door. He smiled at me.

"Aunt Charlotte getting under your skin?" he asked.

"Like a tick," I said, and he laughed.

"I came out to wish you good luck today," he said. "I can't wait to hear all about it."

"Thanks," I said. I felt like fanning my face and imagined smoke pouring out of my ears. He wheeled along beside me as I walked to the door.

"Wait," he said when I opened the door and started to close it behind me. He wheeled out onto the portico. "I like watching you walk."

"What?" I started to smile.

"You have such perfect posture and you glide along as if you're always on some runway modeling clothes or something."

"You're embarrassing me. You just haven't seen that many girls, Evan."

"I've seen enough," he said, his eyes fixed firmly and full of conviction. "On television, over the computer, out there," he said, nodding at the road in front of the estate. "I've seen enough to know you're someone special, Rose. Don't let any rich, spoiled girl at school make you feel inferior. None of them can hold a candle to the fire you have," he added. He spun on his chair and wheeled himself back into the house with two swift motions, as if he had dared say something and wanted to flee from my reaction.

The door closed.

I smiled to myself and suddenly became very conscious of the way I walked down the steps to the waiting automobile.

"Good morning, Miss," Ames said.

"Good morning, Ames. It's a beautiful day, isn't it?" I asked, gazing at the sky and the magnificent grounds for the first time this morning.

"Rather," he said and closed my door for me. Moments later, I was being driven to my new school and wondering what else lay ahead on this highway full of surprises.

The school certainly turned out to be one of them. Charlotte had never said it was a parochial school called Heart of the Angel. Of course, I had never attended a parochial school either. When Ames pulled up in front of the building, I sat in the car and stared at the front steps and the statues of the angels on both sides of the main entrance, which was two wide, tall glass doors above which were the words HEART OF THE ANGEL embossed in granite.

Dozens of students were heading up the stairs. The girls all wore white blouses and blue skirts and the boys were in dark slacks, white shirts, and black ties. None of the boys had very long hair. Most looked like military-style haircuts.

"Miss?" Ames asked after he had opened the door for me and waited a few long moments for me to step out.

"I didn't know this was a religious school," I said as I emerged.

Ames looked at the building as if he hadn't thought about that either.

"One and one is two wherever it's taught," he muttered. "I'll be out here at three-thirty," he added and closed the door.

I watched him drive off and then hesitantly started up the stairs. Because I wasn't in uniform, I attracted attention. The moment I entered the lobby of the building, however, a short, very slim girl with a tight mouth and small, dark eyes approached me with her right hand extended. All of her features were small, nearly childlike. My hand was not big, but hers looked lost within my closed fingers.

"Hi," she said, "I'm Carol Way English, your big sister."

"Big sister?"

The idea that this diminutive girl was anyone's big sister seemed amusing.

"It means I'm going to help you get oriented quickly. First," she said, attempting to be perfect in speech and manners, "we'll go to the office and get your class assignments, and then we'll go to Miss Watson's and she'll fit you with your uniform."

She looked down.

"You're supposed to wear black shoes. Weren't you told?"

"I wasn't told anything," I said.

"Pardon me?"

"I didn't know I was going to a religious school," I said.

She looked skeptical, her smile hinging the corners of her small mouth, stretching her lips and widening the nostrils of her too perfect nose. I suspected cosmetic surgery.

She laughed as if I had said something very funny and shook her head.

"Just follow me. Your name is Rose?"

"Yes."

"You don't exactly have rose-colored hair."

"I wasn't named after my hair. My father liked the name. He thought it was cheerful. Roses usually bring people happiness. He liked to quote that line from Shakespeare about a rose by any other name smelling as sweet."

"You're kidding?" she said, shaking her head, and then continued down the hallway to the bank of offices.

I was rushed along, given my schedule, a building

map, school rules, and a letter from the guidance counselor about how to behave in class so as to get the most out of your lessons and how to do your homework. Don't sit in front of the television set when doing your homework. Get a good night's sleep so you'll be alert every day. *Does anyone really read this?* I wondered.

I was fitted for a uniform, but I didn't see why size even mattered. The blouse I was to wear looked two sizes too big on me and the ankle length skirt wrapped like a blanket around my hips. Again I was told to come in black shoes the next day. I think if Mrs. Watson could, she would have dyed the shoes I was wearing. She made me feel as if I had dressed obscenely.

The classes were much smaller than any I had attended in my previous schools. The students seemed more afraid to be caught misbehaving. Teachers merely had to look angry or disapproving, and whoever was causing even the slightest disturbance became an obedient, polite, and attentive student. Carol Way English had quickly explained to me that students here could be asked to leave and their parents would lose the tuition money.

Before I was brought to my first class, I had to meet with Sister Howell, whose welcome to my new school consisted entirely of a review of the rules that she made sound like the Ten Commandments. When she smiled at the end of her lecture, it was like stamping a smile on the outside of an envelope. She flashed it and then quickly returned her face to that stern look.

The speed with which I was entered, dressed,

warned, and delivered to my first class made my head spin. My teachers were all very nice and concerned, however, and each took some class time to review where I was in my studies and what I needed to do in order to catch up.

Carol Way English introduced me to all my teachers and to other students, never failing to explain, "Her father named her after a flower that brings happiness." Her eyes filled with laughter when she added, "By any other name, she would smell as sweet." Some of the other students laughed, too, but most looked downright bored. At lunch and during the few minutes we had to move from one classroom to another, I was interrogated like some prisoner of war. Everyone wanted to know where I was from, where I now lived, and what my parents did. There was very little reaction or interest until I let it be known that my father had recently died in an accident.

My best class of the day turned out to be my last class, physical education—not that I was any sort of female jock. We were given uniforms for that, too. The teacher, Miss Anderson, had just begun a unit in dance. She was teaching everyone the swing, and it was great fun. The warm-up exercises were, she explained, the same used by professional dancers, ballerinas included. I had not had any sort of dance instruction, of course. Anything I knew, I had picked up on my own.

Miss Anderson asked me to come to her office as soon as I was dressed. She was my youngest teacher, probably not more than in her mid- to late twenties, tall with long legs. She had a softness in her light-blue eyes that put me at ease immediately. I liked her smile. It was the kind that made you feel comfortable, welcome. So many of the teachers I had in my previous schools, and in this one, seemed in a defensive posture, just waiting for their students to misbehave or not pay attention or care about their subjects. There was always tension.

Miss Anderson, who let it be known that her first name was Julie, even though I was not to call her that in school, looked like she really enjoyed her work from the start of the class to the end. She had patches of tiny light brown freckles on the crests of her cheeks and naturally bright orange lips. She kept her reddish-brown hair short, but it had been cut with some style and kept a bit wavy.

"You have a lot of natural rhythm," she told me almost immediately. "Have you had some formal dance instruction?"

"No," I said, almost laughing at the idea.

"I did," she said. "For a long time, I thought I was actually going to be a professional dancer. I was even in some shows, but I didn't have the temperament for that sort of life, I guess. What do you want to be?" she asked. No one else had, not even the headmistress.

"I don't know. I thought about modeling," I said. It was funny. I didn't know her at all, but just her way, her sincerity, put me at ease enough to tell her what I hadn't told anyone else: my fantasy.

"You could do that," she said without the least bit of discouragement. "I've always wanted to do a unit in interpretive dance, but I've been afraid to try. I've helped the drama teacher sometimes when he needed some dancing in his musicals and I do our spring variety show. I still keep my finger in the dream," she added. "If you want, stop by after school one day and we'll try some things," she said.

I nodded even though I didn't know what she meant or what I would do.

It was a good finish to my first day, however. All day long I vowed to burst into the house when Ames drove me back, and start screaming at Charlotte and even Mommy. How dare they put me in a parochial school without telling me? My meeting with Miss Anderson had a calming effect. I wasn't as furious when I entered the house.

Mommy and Charlotte were on the patio drinking from what looked like martini glasses. I heard Mommy's laughter first.

"Hi, Rose. How was your first day at the new school?" she asked immediately. I saw from the blush in her cheeks that she had already drunk more than one of whatever it was in that glass.

"It's a parochial school," I replied, finding myself angrier about her drinking than the deception.

"So? You'll get a better education," Charlotte said.

"Why didn't you tell me?"

She shook her head.

"I didn't see why that was important. You don't

have to become a nun, just listen to what they say and your teachers tell you," she said. "Most of the substantial people I know around here want their children in Heart of the Angel, if they're not already in it."

"Did you know about this, Mommy?" I asked. "I mean, Monica?"

I could see from the expression on her face that she had.

"Why didn't you tell me?"

"I didn't want you to have any preconceived bad feelings," she recited.

I glanced at Charlotte, sensing those were her words she had planted on Mommy's tongue.

"We never kept secrets from each other before," I said.

"It wasn't a secret, really," Charlotte said.

"I was talking to Monica," I said. I looked at Mommy. Her eyes shifted away guiltily.

Charlotte's slow smile lit up her dark eyes with a sinister glow.

"If you don't want to go there, we'll enroll you in the public school, but you'll be in crowded classes and you'll get an inferior education. My goodness, you don't have all that much longer to go before you graduate, Rose," she continued. "Any other girl would be grateful."

"I'm not worried. I know I'll survive," I said, "but my mother and I don't keep things from each other, or hadn't before now."

"I'm sorry, Rose," Mommy said.

Charlotte started to speak, but I quickly snapped, "I'm sorry, too."

Then I turned and walked back into the house.

Moments later, I heard their laughter again and the clink of glasses.

The way it resounded in my heart, it was as if they had clinked them against my bones.

8

Barry

"Did you know I was being sent to a parochial school?" I asked Evan when I went to see him after I had spoken to Mommy and Charlotte.

"Sure," he said. "Why, didn't you?"

"No."

I sat on his bed. He was at his computer, but had stopped whatever he was doing and wheeled toward me.

"What was it like?" he asked, and I described the building, the teachers, and some of the students. I guess I really sounded happy about Miss Anderson and her excitement about dancing.

"I told you there was something magical in the way you moved," he declared. "It doesn't surprise me that she saw it, too, after only an hour. Maybe you should really think about becoming a professional dancer."

"I don't know. Right now, I feel like I'm in some

sort of limbo and can't imagine what I'll be doing next week, much less the rest of my life."

"You look very upset," Evan said.

I revealed how disappointed and angry I was at Mommy for not confiding in me.

"Your aunt is a bad influence," I complained. "My mother would never have done such a thing before we came here."

He didn't laugh. He nodded, thoughtful.

"She's tenacious, like a bulldog until she gets what she wants. I tried to help my mother. She was good at ignoring her when she could, but she was no match for Aunt Charlotte's persistence. My mother was too nice to argue or disagree and she always believed Aunt Charlotte had her best interests and mine at heart anyway.

"I've gotten so her words just float over me. I know it drives her mad. Try to ignore her. Do what you want anyway," he advised.

He asked about the schoolwork and I described some of what I had to do to catch up. It amazed me how much he knew about my senior class subjects and he had all sorts of suggestions and helpful places to research on the Internet.

In the days and weeks that followed, I often did my homework with him. We would listen to music he downloaded over the computer and do my math and science problems. With his skills I had the world's best libraries practically at my fingertips—or his, I should say.

Barry came on Saturday to take me to dinner, as he had promised. We had spoken on the phone a number of times during the week. I could tell from the way he held back when I asked that I had been a topic of discussion at school for a while. What he didn't tell me until we met was how many arguments he had had and the trouble he had gotten himself into defending me.

Mommy and Charlotte had left for Atlanta before Barry's arrival on Saturday. Evan was very nervous about meeting him. On Friday, he told me not to bother bringing him to his room for an introduction.

"He's not here to see me," he said, "and I'll only present a problem for you. How do you explain me and all? Why bother coming up with anything? Just go out and have a good time," he said, but I wouldn't hear of it.

"Barry's very nice, Evan. You'll see," I said, but he was so nervous about it that he kept his door closed on Saturday and pretended to be asleep when the hour of Barry's arrival drew closer.

I was happier to see Barry than I realized I would be. It was as though he brought with him all the good memories I had from the one place we had been for the longest time, a place I could call home. When he drove up, I ran out to embrace him. He kissed me on the cheek, but I held onto him and he looked into my eyes, smiled, and then kissed me again softly on the lips.

"Hi," he said, happy with my big greeting. "It's good to see you, Rose. You look great."

He pulled back and drank in the house and the grounds.

"Wow!" he said. "A lot different from where you were last, huh?"

"A lot different in a lot of ways. C'mon," I said, grabbing his hand and leading him up the stairs and into the house. Of course, he was impressed with the size of the rooms and the elegant rich furnishings, the art and the statues. I quickly explained that my mother had gone to Atlanta with Charlotte.

"But I want you to meet Charlotte's nephew," I said, "before we go out to dinner."

I had told him about Evan's handicap, but I had emphasized how intelligent he was and how expert on the computer. When we went down to his room, the door was still shut tight. I knocked, waited, and called to him.

"Evan. Barry would like to meet you."

He didn't respond.

"Maybe you shouldn't push it," Barry suggested softly.

I knocked again and waited.

"He's still asleep, I guess," I said. Barry nodded. I glanced back at the shut door, disappointed.

Barry had done his research of the area and knew where to go for dinner. Once we got to the restaurant and sat at our table, I never stopped talking. He listened attentively, nodding and smiling occasionally. When I realized I had barely begun to eat, I stopped talking and he laughed.

"I'm sorry," I said. "I probably ruptured your eardrums."

"No. I loved listening to you. I think the dancing you're doing sounds very exciting. By the way, I don't know if I'd told you I applied to NYU early admissions, but I did, and I've been accepted."

"Oh Barry, that's wonderful. Congratulations. You're still thinking of becoming a lawyer?"

"Yes, but I'm thinking I want to be involved in prosecution, maybe become a U.S. attorney someday."

"You'll be whatever you want, I'm sure."

"So will you," he countered. "I couldn't imagine anyone saying no to you, Rose."

I smiled. I was almost too excited to eat. The food was delicious, but my stomach felt as if I had just gotten off a roller coaster. In the last week I had hit so many peaks and valleys emotionally, I wasn't surprised.

Barry talked about some of the other kids I had been somewhat friendly with, excluding Paula, of course. Every time I brought up her name, he tried to change the subject. Finally, he told me about some of the arguments he had had and the fight he had gotten into with Ed Wiley, which had resulted in his being in detention for a week.

"Oh, no. You were such good friends. I hate to be the cause of anything like that."

"You weren't. It was all Paula's fault. Let's just talk about good things from now on, Rose," he said quickly, letting me believe there were even more gruesome and ugly details.

After dinner we rode back to the house slowly. I could sense he was prolonging his time with me. I didn't want him to leave either. I suggested he come in and maybe we would find Evan up. We didn't. His door remained shut and when I knocked again, we got the same silent response. It wasn't that late yet, so we went into the family room and started watching some television, sitting beside each other on the long settee.

We began to kiss, small, exploratory kisses, our lips grazing our faces, his moving over my eyes, my nose, and always finding their way back to mine. I turned into him and moaned softly.

He chanted my name as if it was a prayer, and he told me how much he had missed me and longed to see me. His hands moved up from my waist to my shoulders and then over my breasts. It felt good to be loved, to be wanted, to be needed. I said nothing when he reached back and shut off the lamp beside us. Only the glow of the television screen cast any illumination over us. It was a warm light, making his face glow. When he undid the buttons of my blouse and slipped it off my shoulders, he brought his lips down to follow the lines of my neck to my shoulders and kissed me again while he took my blouse off completely. I could feel him fumbling with my bra clip and reached back to undo it myself. He nudged it away with the tip of his nose and began to kiss my breasts.

Excitement within me spiraled out, reaching every part of my body, right down to my toes. I had no idea how far we would go. I toyed with complete abandon and he went further and further, moving his hands up my legs, over my thighs, until he made my heart nearly leap out of my chest.

"We'd better stop," I whispered in his ear, even

though I didn't want to stop. I almost wished he would ignore me, but he was too sweet and loving not to listen. He held me tightly, waiting for his own breathing to calm.

"My heart's pounding like some sledgehammer," he said.

"I'm afraid they'll come home and walk in on us, Barry."

"No, you're right," he said. "Of course."

"I don't want you to be upset," I said and kissed him. He kissed me back.

"When you go beyond a certain point, it's like trying to stop a car on ice," he muttered. He kissed my breasts again and held me just as tightly. "It's hard to just stop," he said, not moving away. "Maybe if we do it slowly, like easing out of quicksand."

"You think I'm quicksand?"

"I wouldn't mind if you were pulling me down and into you, Rose," he said.

I smiled and kissed him. He moved down, his lips traveling over my breasts again to my stomach and to my skirt, which was still undone. I pressed my hands against his ears and felt myself being pulled along as he went further and further until I gasped.

"Please," I said with barely a breath.

"All right. I'm sorry. I want you so much," he said.

We lay next to each other, waiting for our blood to settle, like water that had reached its boiling point. All we could hear was the sound of our own deep breathing. Then, I heard something in the hallway and moved quickly to get my bra back on and my blouse.

"Are they here?" he asked nervously. He reached over to turn the lamp on.

We both listened. Except for the very low murmur of the television, it was silent again. I rose slowly and went to the door. I thought I heard the squeaking sound of Evan's wheelchair and then the nearly silent closing of his door. My heart pounded. Had he seen us?

"Rose? Anyone there?"

"No," I said.

"Maybe I should get going," Barry said, coming up beside me. He kissed me on the cheek and I leaned back into him while he held me, kissed my hair, and whispered, "I really like you, Rose. I like you a lot."

"I'm glad, Barry," I said. I turned to him and we kissed again. Then we walked to the front door.

We stood outside looking up at the starry night sky. There was no moon but the stars seemed closer, their illumination washing the world in a silvery glow that turned the trees into sentinels manning the walls of our castle, keeping all the sadness and worry away from us, securing our dreams. It was magical.

"I'll call you tomorrow," Barry promised.

"Good."

He kissed me again and then he left, letting his hand slide slowly through mine. I kept mine extended as if the warmth and the feel of his remained, even though he was already down the stairs. He paused at his car, waved again, and got in. I watched him drive off. Then I embraced myself and went back into the house.

I stood in the foyer and listened. The television was still on, but I didn't see or hear Evan. I returned to the family room, straightened out the settee, and then turned off the set. Before I went upstairs, I walked quietly toward Evan's room. I noticed that his door was slightly ajar and there was some light behind it, a flickering glow.

"Evan?" I said at the door. He didn't reply. I nudged it open a bit more and gazed in. At first what I saw seemed so strange, I thought I was imagining it. He was at his computer, wearing his headphones—and nothing else. For a moment I couldn't breathe. I stepped back, closed the door as quietly as I could, and fled up the corridor, up the stairs, and into my room.

Whatever he was doing, I thought, I had no right to spy on him and certainly no right to judge him. I pushed the images out of my mind, quickly replacing them with images of Barry and sounds of his voice, his words, our wonderful lovemaking.

I had wanted to be as intimate as possible with him, but I didn't want him thinking that if I was that intimate with him so quickly, I might be the same with other boys. It has to be special; it's important that it's special. It won't have the same meaning and significance if it isn't, I thought.

But I was certain in my heart that we would be complete lovers soon. I fell asleep dreaming of that and the wonder of what just the thought of it did to the way I saw and felt about everything around me. It was as if all my senses had been heightened and my blood made richer. The tips of my fingers and toes tingled with expectation. I moaned softly to myself, hugged my pillow, and pressed my cheek to the soft fluffiness, anxious to travel quickly through the dark doors of sleep into the wonder of my fantasies.

Just before dawn, I woke with a start. It felt like someone had nudged my shoulder with his or her forefinger. I sat up and listened. The house was dead quiet, but I thought about Mommy. What time did they return? I had not heard a sound. Was I in that deep of a sleep? Too curious to fall back to sleep, I rose, put on my robe, and quietly made my way out and to Mommy's room. The door was shut, but I opened it very quietly and peered in at her bed. There was enough light pouring through the window to see it outlined and to clearly see that she was not in it, that she had not been in it.

My heart did a flip. Where was she? I closed the door and listened and then returned to my bedroom, but I was unable to fall asleep. I lay there listening for someone. I finally heard the maid moving about downstairs, so I rose, washed, and dressed as quickly as I could. When I descended, she was preparing the breakfast table.

"Good morning, Nancy Sue," I said, trying to hide my anxiety.

"Morning, Miss."

"Have you spoken with Mrs. Curtis already?" I asked.

She looked at me as if I had asked her if she had been to the moon.

"No, Miss."

"I just wondered," I said. I went outside and walked to the garage where I saw the car. If the car was back, where was Mommy?

I went in and to Evan's room, knocking on his door.

"Evan? Are you up yet?"

"Yes," he said and opened the door. He was dressed and in his wheelchair. "I thought I'd come out for breakfast today. Did you have a good time last night?"

"Yes, Evan. Why wouldn't you answer when I knocked? I wanted you to meet Barry and he really did want to meet you very much."

"I wasn't in the mood for company," he said quickly and wheeled himself into the hallway. "Did you have breakfast already?"

"No."

"Good. You can tell me about your evening, if you want," he said.

"Wait."

He paused and looked at me, puzzled by my tone.

"My mother," I said.

"What about her?"

"She's not back. The car is back, but she isn't."

"Oh." He smiled and looked up as if he could see through the ceiling. "Auntie Charlotte's work, I'm sure," he said.

"What do you mean?"

He started to wheel himself toward the dining room. I followed quickly.

"Evan? What did you mean?"

"I told you how she was always trying to fix my mother up with someone, arranging dates. Maybe she thinks she's Cupid," he said and turned sharply into the dinning room. "Good morning, Nancy Sue. I'm starving today. How about some eggs and grits?"

"Very good, Master Evan."

"Just call me Evan, Nancy Sue. I've asked you a hundred times. I'm past being a master this or that," he lectured. She looked more amused than upset and left to prepare his food.

"What are you saying, Evan?" I demanded.

He shrugged.

"She went to a party where my aunt Charlotte introduced her to some fine gentlemen or gentleman, and you say she's not back. It's not rocket science, Rose."

"My mother isn't like that," I said, shaking my head.

"My mother wasn't either," he said. "But here I am." He gazed out the window. "Here I am."

More frightened than furious, I spun on my heels and marched down the hallway and up the stairs. I went to Charlotte's closed door and knocked. I heard her groan so I knocked again.

"What is it?" she cried.

I opened the door and stepped into her bedroom. She was still in bed, the comforter drawn to her chin. With the netting over her hair and her pale face peering over the blanket at me, she looked like some sort of space creature.

"What is it? Something happen to Evan?"

"No. Where's my mother?"

"Oh," she said. She struggled to get herself into a sitting position and reached for a glass of water before responding. "She's not in her room?"

"No."

She smiled.

"She'll be back soon, I suppose," she replied.

"What do you mean? What happened to her?"

"Nothing she didn't want to happen to her, I expect. She and Grover enjoyed each other's company far more than even I had anticipated. She accepted an invitation to see his family's Atlanta apartment and they left the party. I waited for them to return, but," she said with a smile, "she didn't."

"Are you saying my mother spent the night with a man she has just met?"

"Your mother is a grown woman, Rose. Don't you think you're being a bit overly dramatic about this? She's still a young woman. Let her enjoy what's left of her youth and beauty.

"What she or any woman in her state doesn't need is an anchor tied to her legs in the form of a neurotic daughter."

"I'm not a neurotic daughter!"

"Good. Then all will be well. Would you please ask Nancy Sue to bring me some black coffee and some ice water? Thank you," she said, lowering herself back under her comforter. She closed her eyes to indicate that the conversation was at an absolute end.

I stared at her, fuming, and then left, closing the door a bit too hard, for I heard her groan in dismay.

Mommy didn't return until late in the afternoon. Evan and I were out on the rear patio. I was reading and talking about *Hamlet* with him because it was a play my class had already done and I had to read and understand quickly. He had gone on the Internet and printed out some very helpful study guides, and he had read the play himself. His understanding of the language and the metaphors amazed me. Sometimes when he spoke or explained something I had missed, he sounded like my teacher at school. I told him so. I could see he was proud and enjoyed the compliment.

"You see, Evan. You do have a lot to offer people. You've got to stop living like a hermit, an electronic hermit with your computer as your only window to the world. You've got to interact with people, too."

"People disappoint me too often," he said.

"So? You'll meet other people who won't."

He stared at me for a moment and then nodded.

"Tell me about our father," he requested. "I mean, really tell me everything. I want to know the silliest, smallest details about him."

"Okay," I said. Despite it all, I loved talking about Daddy. I closed my eyes and brought up the visions of him I most cherished. I described his gestures, his smile, the cologne he wore, his funny expressions, some of the impulsive things he had done and would do. I went on and on and when I gazed at Evan, I saw a soft smile on his lips.

"The way you make him sound, I can almost understand why my mother became involved with a married man. He was a snake-charmer. I guess, if I had met him, I would have been forced to like him myself, even though I wouldn't approve of him."

"I think so, Evan."

"Thanks," he said and sat back. That was when we heard Mommy's laughter and voice.

He looked at me sharply.

"Don't make her feel like a sinner," he warned. "I did that to my mother sometimes, and I've always regretted it."

"I just want to know exactly what's going on here," I said, jumping up.

I heard all the conversation coming from the living room and hurried to it, where I found Charlotte sitting across from Mommy and a tall, dark-haired man with a mustache like Clark Gable, a strong square chin, high cheekbones, and a dazzling pair of the most beautiful hazel eyes I had ever seen. He was long-legged and trim and wore a dark blue blazer and a pair of light blue slacks with blue boat shoes.

"This must be Rose," he said before I could speak.

"Yes, it is," Mommy said. "Hi, honey. I'd like you to meet Mr. Fleming."

"Please, call me Grover," he said, rising. He extended his hand. I glanced at it and at Mommy and then shook it, letting go so quickly anyone would have thought his was full of thorns. Charlotte was beaming from her chair.

"Hello," I said, forcing the word through my tight throat.

Nancy Sue entered with a tray, carrying three glasses of champagne.

"Ah, wonderful," Grover declared. He handed Mommy hers and I saw by the way she looked up at him that she was lost in his eyes. It made my heart deflate like a balloon. Charlotte took hers.

"Thank you, Nancy Sue. Rose, would you like anything?" she asked sweetly enough to make my stomach churn.

"No, thank you," I said quickly.

"How was your date, honey?" Mommy asked.

"Very nice," I said. "I tried to wait up for you."

"Where's Evan?" Charlotte quickly asked.

"On the patio. We were studying *Hamlet* together."

"Ah, to be or not to be...for me, there is no longer a question," Grover declared, his eyes on Mommy, who looked like an adoring teenager. He tapped her glass with his.

"Why don't you see if you can talk poor Evan into going to a movie this afternoon?" Charlotte suggested. She turned to Grover. "The child either has his nose in a book or his eyes glued to a computer screen. He doesn't get out of the house."

"Oh?" He turned to me and smiled. "If anyone can get him out, I'll bet it's you, Rose," he said and laughed a tight, small laugh that made my nerves tremble. Mommy looked like she enjoyed every breath he took.

Couldn't she see how smooth he was? He slid around the room with his eyes, his gestures, and his smile like some eel, titillating both Charlotte and Mommy. He used his good looks well, with confidence, even arrogance.

"Don't worry about us," Charlotte continued. "We're going to a dinner party."

"Another dinner party?" I blurted, looking at Mommy.

"Yes," she said, exploding with excitement. "Isn't it wonderful?"

I looked at Grover, whose eyes were on me, darker, more expectant and analytical, waiting for my reaction. Charlotte was her usual smug self.

"I don't know, Monica," I said with words sharp enough to cut ears, "is it?"

I turned and left the room. Charlotte and Grover's laughter felt like small rocks thrown at my back. Evan took one look at me when I returned to the patio and simply said, "Uh-oh."

I didn't respond. I kept marching off the patio and down the path, my head down, my heart thumping.

Evan wheeled himself behind me and caught up when I reached his tree. He didn't speak. He watched me sulk for a few long moments.

"I like being with you," I finally said, "and I wanted to get to know you very much, but I think living here is a big mistake."

"It's hard, I guess, to see your mother with some other man. You keep thinking about your father. I didn't have that problem," he added, "but I didn't like her being with anyone anyway. I guess I had the old Oedipus complex, huh?"

"I don't mind her finding someone else. I don't want her pining away in some attic, dying like an old, frustrated widow," I said sharply. "That's not it, but..."

"But what?"

"I don't know." I shook my head. I didn't know exactly. I looked down at him. His eyes were intense, glued to my face.

"There's something not right."

He smiled.

"Something's rotten in the state of Denmark," he said, quoting one of the lines from *Hamlet* we had just discussed.

"Exactly," I said. I looked back at the house. "Exactly."

9

Dancing

In the months that followed, Mommy's social life continued to grow. There were strings of days when we didn't even see each other, and if there were some dead spots, some days or nights when it appeared there were no dinners to attend, no shows to see, no art galleries and openings to appear at, Charlotte always managed to come up with something for them to do, some additional shopping, some elaborate lunch. She bought Mommy more clothes, more costume jewelry, more shoes. They traded outfits. They became almost inseparable.

Maybe out of anger or out of frustration and nervousness, I devoted myself to my studies and to the dance lessons Miss Anderson conducted. Soon, it was just the two of us remaining after school. She told me she was a frustrated choreographer and loved the idea that she now had a student with whom or on whom she could experiment. Her idol was Bob Fosse. She had videotapes of his work that we watched together. When she explained and demonstrated something and I tried it, she was always pleased.

"You've got something, Rose," she said. "You pick all of it up so easily, and you've got the looks and the legs. Think seriously about this," she advised.

Evan was very supportive and very excited for me. He decided we should create a dance studio and had Nancy Sue and Ames clear everything out of the guest bedroom down the hall from his room. He even ordered some large wall mirrors to be installed. Charlotte didn't oppose it or even acknowledge it with much more than a simple, "How delightful, Rose. You're getting him interested in something other than himself and his dreary computer."

When Mommy learned about it, she recited almost the exact words, but she rarely stopped by to see me practice. Evan would spend hours with me, sitting in his wheelchair and watching me go through the warm-up exercises and routines.

"Doesn't all this repetition bore you, Evan?" I asked him. He shook his head vigorously.

"No. It's like I'm moving through you, with you. You're my legs. I love it," he declared.

That made me feel good about it, and soon I was able to forget that he was there, that his eyes were fixed on every muscle movement clearly visible in my tights.

Barry returned every Saturday he could to take me to a movie or to dinner, sometimes just to enjoy a picnic on the grounds, but he still hadn't met Charlotte, nor had Mommy been around when he had arrived. Their weekends were always filled with social activities in and around Atlanta.

Finally, Evan consented to meet him. I couldn't help being nervous for both of them, but to my delight, Barry knew more about computers than I had anticipated. Once their conversation turned to that, they were both at it around Evan's computer and I felt like a third wheel on my own date. They took great delight in showing each other different Internet sites and showing each other shortcuts.

"Excuse me," I said, "but weren't we talking about going to the movies tonight after we had something quick to eat? What are we supposed to eat, a health bar?" I asked with my hands on my hips, nodding at the clock.

"Oh," Barry said. "Sorry."

I laughed.

"It's all right. I just started to feel lonely," I said, and they both laughed, after which Evan immediately looked guilty for stealing Barry away.

"Sorry," he said, too.

"There's nothing for you to apologize for, Evan. Why don't you come out with us?" I suggested.

It put such terror in his eyes, he couldn't respond for a moment. He looked at Barry and at me and started to shake his head.

"I know your wheelchair folds up and goes in the car trunk, so don't use that as an excuse," I warned.

"Sure," Barry said. "Come along with us. You'll love this movie."

"I can't. I..."

"Have a date on the Internet?" I punched at him. He turned crimson. "I'm sorry," I said quickly. "I didn't mean..."

"No, no, it's all right. I did promise to chat with someone, but..."

"You'll come along?" Barry asked.

Evan looked at me.

"Please come, Evan," I pleaded, and he took a breath and nodded.

"Okay."

"Great."

"I've got to prepare a bit," he said.

"We'll wait for you in the living room," I said and Barry and I left him.

"Thanks for doing that, Barry," I said.

"He's great. No problem," Barry told me, and I kissed him.

It turned out to be a wonderful evening. Evan's interest and excitement in everything we did and saw made both Barry and me feel good. It was almost like taking a child out and watching him experience things you took for granted.

When we came home, I made us all hot chocolate with whipped cream and we sat around and talked about the movie for a while. Then Evan, looking at me first, excused himself, thanking Barry, and wheeled to his room to let us have some time together. Barry stayed later than ever. I was concerned for him, but he insisted. When we began to kiss, I took his hand and stood up, leading him out of the living room, up the stairs, and into my bedroom.

"The ice is a lot more slippery in here, Rose," he said when I sat on my bed and still held his hand. "Stopping might be impossible."

"I'm not afraid," I said. "I'd slide anywhere with you."

He laughed and knelt down before me, putting his head on my lap while I stroked his hair.

"You're trembling," I said, feeling it.

"In anticipation," he replied.

He stood up slowly, leaned over to kiss me, and we started to make love.

"You're so beautiful, Rose," he said, "but you're so casual and down to earth, you make me feel comfortable. People say beauty is only skin-deep, but it's not true with you. Yours is inside and out. I can't imagine caring for anyone more than I care for you. I love you so much, it makes my heart ache and stops me cold wherever I am and whatever I'm doing. I must look stupid with this silly smile on my face, seeing your face before me no matter who or what is in front of me."

"I hope you look stupid forever and ever then," I said. He laughed and held me for a moment before bringing his lips to mine and then slowly, in graceful motions, helping me take off my clothing and taking off his. "I came prepared," he whispered. "Just in case we found ourselves on the ice."

"Slide," I urged him.

Daddy used to say that if you build something up

too much, no matter how wonderful it is, you'll be disappointed.

"Keep a lid on your expectations, Rose. Take things slowly, enjoy the surprises."

I tried so hard not to expect bells ringing or feel myself floating on clouds, all the things I read in books. This was my reality, my entrance into womanhood. Anyone could have sex anytime, but to have it with love was what I was longing for and hoping would happen. It was the only dream I permitted, the one expectation I would not deny myself.

And it was all that I had imagined it would be. We were gentle with each other and loving. We did feel connected, a part of each other in a deeper way. It seemed to me we tasted each other's very souls, and when it was over, we held onto each other to prolong the moment and put it forever and ever indelibly on the very face of our hearts.

When Barry and I stepped out of my bedroom, we walked right into Charlotte coming up the stairs. She paused, a wide, salacious smile on her face. Mommy was not with her.

"Is this your boyfriend from the past?" she asked.

Barry looked nervously at me.

"No. He's my boyfriend from the present. Barry Burton, this is Charlotte Alden Curtis."

"Hello," Barry said.

"Is Rose giving you a tour of the house?"

She laughed and continued up the stairs.

"Don't wait up for your mother," she said as she passed me.

I felt the blood rush into my face and quickly continued down the stairs. Without a word, I walked out of the house.

"What did she mean?" Barry asked.

"My mother is enjoying the social life Charlotte has found for her. She seems to take pleasure in my uneasiness about it," I said, firing a hot look back at the doorway.

"Will you be all right?"

"Yes," I said. "Don't worry, Barry."

He nodded and then kissed me good night. I watched him leave and looked toward the darkness that closed in around his car, wondering where Mommy would be spending the night tonight and what would become of us.

All the next day, Mommy's behavior and new lifestyle gnawed at me. At dance practice, Miss Anderson immediately saw something was bothering me.

"You're missing beats, Rose," she said. We were rehearsing for the spring variety show. I was going to do an interpretive dance she had choreographed. "Something wrong?"

At first I shook my head and just started dancing again. Then I stopped and started to cry. It was as if my tears had control of me. I couldn't stop them and I couldn't stop shaking.

Miss Anderson put her arm around me and led me to the chair.

"Can I help you?" she asked.

I swallowed the heavy throat lump and took a deep breath.

"No," I said. "It's not something anyone can help, I guess."

"Try me," she pleaded.

I told her about Mommy and how she had changed so much. She listened with a look of concern, nodding occasionally with understanding.

"Maybe you don't realize how lost she was after your father's passing, Rose. She had to find a way out of her pain, too."

"She's just so changed," I moaned.

"Great events change you sometimes," Miss Anderson said. She went on to tell me how she had been a very shy girl most of her life. She revealed that she had an older sister who had died from Hodgkin's disease.

"She was beautiful and bright and well on her way to becoming a dancer, too. She was like you, born with natural rhythm, graceful, with the ability to touch people's hearts and souls through her dancing. When she died, it broke my mother and father's hearts. I felt an obligation to fill her shoes and smothered my shyness. I had to wash the gloom out of their eyes. Great events change you," she repeated.

"I guess," I said, wiping my cheeks.

"Your mother will be fine," she said. "Give her a chance. She won't forget who you are and who she is to you, I'm sure."

I nodded and smiled.

"Thanks."

"I can't have my star being sad unless it's part of the dance," she declared, and I laughed. "Ready?"

"Yes."

I was back at it and much better. During the months that followed, I continued to practice at home for Evan and, occasionally, when Barry arrived early on the weekends, I danced for him as well. They were a great audience, boosting my confidence with their clapping and howling.

Evan went out with us more often, sometimes just for a ride, sometimes to eat and go to a movie. We took him shopping at the mall as well, where he and Barry pondered over new computer software products. Often, I would be sitting outside the store, waiting for them. Beside me on the benches were husbands who had brought their wives and were patiently waiting as well. It made me laugh to see the expressions on their faces when they realized I was the one waiting for my boyfriend and my half-brother to shop until they dropped and not the other way around.

The spring variety show was coming upon us fast, and with every passing day, every new morning that I woke and realized how close we were, my heart increased the speed of its beat. It got so I was almost frozen in my bed, afraid to start my day at school. I saw my name up on the posters in the hallways, heard my teachers talking among themselves. They were all telling me how much they were looking forward to my performance. Miss Anderson wasn't sparing any adjectives describing me, it seemed. I begged her not to blow me up so high in everyone's eyes.

"I'll never meet their expectations," I cried.

"They'd have to be total clods," she replied. "Stop worrying. You can't help being who and what you are, Rose. I can feel it," she declared with such drama, I was mesmerized. "Stopping it would be like trying to hold back the sun."

Her words took my breath away and filled me with exaltation. Soon I was eating, breathing, sleeping dance. I would wake up in the morning exhausted and imagined that I had gotten up and dance-walked instead of sleepwalked.

I don't know how many times I reminded Mommy about the upcoming performance, but I was terrified she wouldn't show up because she would have some social obligation or another. She was still seeing Grover Fleming. Every time she mentioned his name to me, I held my breath, anticipating her telling me he had proposed or something, but that didn't come, and I began to wonder if Miss Anderson wasn't right, after all. Mommy was just trying to find herself again and wasn't making any new lifelong commitments.

Finally, the Saturday of the variety show arrived. Barry and I had convinced Evan to go shopping for a new suit. Barry said he would come early in the morning to take him. I pleaded with Evan to do it, claiming it would help me keep my mind off my performance and help me to be less nervous. He had access to credit cards and funds. He was nervous about it, but he truly enjoyed the day with us. Barry helped him try on the clothes and I sat and passed judgment on how he looked. He was so shy and embarrassed, his face was like a red rose most of the time, but in the end, I could see the pleasure in his eyes when he held his packages in his lap. He even agreed to have his hair styled and shortened.

"My two escorts," I declared when we returned to the house that day.

"Your two big fans, you mean," Barry cried.

The three of us laughed. We carried our merriment with us into the house, all three of us ravenously hungry from excitement more than anything, I suppose. However, the moment we entered the house, I could sense that something was different. For one thing, when Nancy Sue saw me, she shifted her eyes away quickly. Even Ames gazed at me longer and then moved along as if he was uncomfortable in my presence.

"You two go ahead," I said to Barry and Evan. "I'll join you in a minute. I want to talk to my mother," I said and hurried up the stairs to her bedroom. The car was still in the garage and Ames was here, so I knew she hadn't left for any social affair with Charlotte. *She better not be planning to do so,* I thought.

The door was closed. I knocked, waited, knocked and called to her.

Charlotte stepped out of her bedroom. She was wearing one of her Armani tuxedo suits.

"Oh, Rose honey, you were gone so long," she said

with her usual syrupy sweetness. "Monica waited and waited as long as she could."

"What? What do you mean, waited? Waited why?"

"To say good-bye, of course," she declared with a wide, gleeful smile.

"Good-bye?" I shook my head. "No. Tonight's the variety show. She didn't go off to one of her social events tonight. No," I insisted and opened the door to find Mommy and prove Charlotte wrong.

Not only wasn't she there, but there was a new sense of emptiness to the room itself. I saw one of the closet doors was nearly half open, revealing naked hangers. The top of her vanity table was cleared. Gone was all her makeup.

I spun around. Charlotte stood in the doorway, gloating.

"Where is she?"

"A wonderful thing has happened," Charlotte said. "Grover has asked her to be with him. They've gone off together."

"Be with him? I don't understand. What does that mean? Marry him?"

"Well, marriage wasn't specifically mentioned," she said. She scrunched her nose. "People today often just run off and live together. It's less intimidating." She pealed off a laugh and turned.

"When is she coming back? Didn't she leave a letter, a note for me?"

"Oh, yes," she said, turning at the top of the stairs. "She did mention a note or something. I think she said she would leave it on your bed. I'm sorry I can't come to your performance tonight, but there's an event for the mayor of Atlanta that I just must attend. Break a leg," she added. It was the traditional good wish for a performer, but in her case, I thought she meant it literally.

She started down the stairway, and I rushed into my room. There was a small envelope on my pillow. I seized it and ripped the envelope impatiently.

Dear Rose,

Please forgive me for not attending your dance recital tonight, but a wonderful thing has happened. Grover has asked me to be with him, to be his special lady. We're off to vacation in Hilton Head, South Carolina. It's sort of a test to see how we'll do around each other night and day. I know we'll do well. I know this seems impulsive, but I remember how your father enjoyed being impulsive. There's something to be said for it. I feel like a young girl again. I feel the sun will shine forever on my face.

Charlotte has promised to look after you and any of your needs. She's really been a great friend to me and she will be to you, I'm sure. She's happy about what you've done for Evan and so am I.

I'll call you as soon as I stop to take a breath. Be happy for me.

Love,
Monica

My fingers weakened and the letter floated out of my hand to the floor. I felt so hollow inside. My muscular new legs lost all their strength and I sank as well. Lying there, I sobbed and sobbed until it hurt.

Because I took so long to meet Barry and Evan, Barry came up to see what was wrong and found me lying on the floor, my eyes closed, my hand now clutching Mommy's note.

"Rose!" he cried, rushing to my side. "What's wrong?"

I sat up slowly and wiped my cheeks. Then I just handed him the note. He read it quickly and looked at me.

"You had no idea this was going to happen today?"

"No," I said. "I always had an aching fear, but I didn't think it was going to happen this fast. And today of all days!"

"I'm sorry," he said, looking at the note. "I know it's hard for you," he added, "but you can't let this spoil your performance, Rose. You've worked too hard."

"How could she do this?"

"I'll be there for you and so will Evan, and we'll clap enough for four people," he promised, to bring a smile back to my dreary face.

I didn't smile but I rose and we went down to have something to eat. Evan took one look at me and knew immediately something very serious had happened. I told him and he, too, told me how sorry he was but how important it was for me not to get myself so depressed that I would ruin my performance.

"The show must go on!" he cried. He and Barry did their best to cheer me up. They clowned around and made jokes, Barry imitating me warming up and Evan pretending he was a stern dance instructor shouting orders.

As the clock ticked closer to the hour at which I would have to prepare myself, I began to understand the concept of stage fright. I wasn't sure I would actually be able to get up and go, much less dance in front of hundreds of people.

"I'm going up to take my bath," I told them. "I need some time alone," I whispered to Barry.

"No problem, Rose. I'll help Evan get himself dressed. We men have to work on ourselves, too," he added in a deliberately loud voice.

I filled the tub and lit a candle. While I soaked, I listened to some soft music and tried to keep myself calm. I couldn't help thinking about Daddy and how carefree he had been about everything in his life. He seemed a man who shrugged off tension and pressure as easily as a duck shook off water. *Didn't I inherit any of that?* I wondered.

Maybe it all caught up with him, I thought. As hard as it was to face, maybe all the pressure and tension he had locked up in some secret place in his heart overflowed finally and he exploded. Maybe he did take his own life.

I could hear him at my side, reciting, "Your eyes are two diamonds. Your hair is spun gold. Your lips are rubies and your skin comes from pearls. My Rose petal."

"Oh, Daddy," I moaned. "Oh, Daddy, I need you now. I've always needed you. Sinner or not, you were my Daddy," I whispered and swallowed back my tears.

Somehow the forces that drive anyone to achieve, to go forward and try to accomplish something significant in his or her life, took over inside me. I fixed my hair and my makeup, dressed, and went down at the appropriate hour. Both Barry and Evan were waiting patiently, both looking very handsome and trying not to look nervous for me.

"You're both very handsome," I said.

"You," Evan said before Barry could get the words out, "look fantastic."

"Ditto," Barry said.

He helped get Evan into his car and we were off, my heart no longer pounding. It was more like a snail that had pulled itself into a shell, the beat so low, I had to put my hand over my breast to see if I was still alive.

The size of the audience made it impossible for me to swallow. I thought I would simply faint at the feet of all these elegantly dressed adults and my classmates. This was surely a super critical audience, rich people who had been to one professional performance after another, I thought, and nearly turned and ran from the auditorium.

Barry took charge of Evan, wheeling him to a place in front of the stage while I went backstage to meet Miss Anderson.

"I can't do this," were the first words out of my mouth.

She looked at me askance, smiled, shook her head, and put her arm around my shoulders to walk me away from the others.

"Do you think I would ask you to do something I knew you couldn't do, Rose?"

"That audience..."

"Will be blown away. You'll see," she promised. "What's the worst that can happen anyway?"

"I'll fall on my face," I said.

She shrugged.

"So you'll pick yourself up and start over while I come out and do a two-step."

That brought a smile to my lips.

"I know you're going to do well. When it's over, I'll have a surprise for you," she said.

"What?"

"If I tell you, it won't be a surprise, now will it? Just go get into your costume and do your warm-up exercises. We're starting the show. You're number five."

She squeezed my hand and left me so she could tend to the others.

Something happened when I walked out and into the spotlight. I wouldn't think about it until much later, when I was alone and after all the applause had long died down, even its echo in my ears. Alone and quiet, I would first realize and remember how Miss Anderson had hugged me when I came off and into the stage wing, how my classmates in the show had gathered around me to congratulate me, some of them so impressed they just wanted to touch me. I would first realize and remember all the people, strangers who came up to me after the show to make a special point of complimenting me. Later I would hear, "You were fantastic. You were wonderful. You were so good you brought me to tears." It was as if all the words, all the accolades had been frozen, put on pause just outside my ears, and then later, when I had a chance to reflect, they were released to flow through my ears.

I couldn't forget Barry's and Evan's faces, however. They were both beaming so brightly, I thought they could light up the whole school. Barry kissed me and Evan reached up to take my hand. I hugged him, too.

"Your mother's a fool for not being here," Evan whispered.

When I had first stepped into the wings about to go onstage, I had thought about Mommy and wished she was out there. I had even imagined her surprising me and showing up. After the performance, she would come rushing backstage to throw her arms around me and cry with happy tears. She would say, "I woke up halfway to Hilton Head and realized I couldn't miss this and am I ever so glad I did."

It was one of those soap-bubble fantasies. Of course, it popped and was gone. She wasn't there.

As soon as I had changed and come out to meet Barry and Evan, Miss Anderson reappeared with a man at her side. He was tall and very elegant looking, but very slim with dark, thin lips and strong dark eyes.

"Rose, I'd like you to meet someone," Miss Anderson said. "He's an old friend of mine."

"Not so old," the man said quickly.

"A good friend of mine," she corrected. "Edmond Senetsky."

"Hi," I said. I was looking for Barry and Evan and gazed past him.

I saw him smile and glance at Miss Anderson.

"I'm not as impressive as I imagined," he told her.

"I didn't tell her anything about you," she explained to him.

He raised his eyebrows.

"Oh?"

"I didn't want to make her any more nervous than she was."

"She didn't seem very nervous to me," he said.

I looked more attentively at him. Who was he?

"Rose, Edmond is a theatrical agent, but more important, he is the son of Madame Senetsky, who runs the famous Senetsky School of Performing Arts in New York. He was visiting one of his clients in Atlanta and I asked him to stop in tonight to see you."

"Oh," I said. *What does this mean?* I wondered.

"I didn't tell you about him because I didn't want you to have any disappointments."

"Very diplomatic of you, Julie," he told her. "You knew I wasn't going to be disappointed."

"I hoped you weren't."

"I trust your eye for talent almost as much as I do

my own," he said. I thought he sounded terribly arrogant. He turned to me.

"I think—no, I *know* my mother would want you to attend her school. You'll remind her of herself," he added with a smile. "She was a dancer as well as an actress. She had classical training, the same sort you'll get in her school."

"I'll get?"

Miss Anderson smiled.

"My mother permits me to choose one student a year for her. It's taken years and years of proving myself to get her to do that," he said.

"You think I should go to her school?" I asked.

"Precisely."

"But..."

"We'll talk about it later, honey. I know you have people waiting for you."

"It's nice to have met you," I said to Edmond.

"Yes, well, if you're smart, and lucky, you'll meet me again," he said.

I thought that was quite odd and quite egotistical, but I didn't say another word. I hurried to join Barry and Evan and bask in the glow of my great success with the two people I loved the most in the world, hoping I wouldn't cry when I thought about Mommy.

Epilogue

In the end I suppose there was more than one reason I decided to go to Madame Senetsky's School of Performing Arts in New York City. I was upset because it was almost a week after the variety show performance before Mommy called me. There was a letdown after the show anyway. All the preparation, practice, dedication had reached a peak. Miss Anderson and I still danced after school, but it wasn't the same, and there was a heavy cloud of depression hovering over me from morning until night. Every time the phone rang, I waited to hear my mother's voice, but I didn't, and I began to wonder if I ever would.

Finally, I did.

"Rose sweetheart, how are you?" Mommy cried.

"I'm all right," I said.

"Tell me about your little show. Was it as successful as you hoped?"

"Yes, Mommy."

"I wish I could have been there. I should have been there," she added, a dark note in her voice that cracked at the end of her sentence.

"Mommy? Are you all right?"

She was silent.

"What's wrong?"

"Oh, Rose, I've been a stupid schoolgirl, it seems," she said, her voice so choked it was only a whisper.

"I don't understand."

"Grover left me this morning. And it was embarrassing, too. He didn't pay the hotel bill."

"What? Why?"

"He got up earlier than I did, and when I went looking for him, I was given a note he had left at the desk. He said he had made a mistake thinking he could be with only one woman. He said he didn't want to hurt me any more, so it was best he just leave."

"Why haven't you come home?"

"I'm too embarrassed. I had to sell some of my jewelry to pay the bill here."

"I'll pack and come to you, Mommy. Tell me where to come."

"No, honey, no. You're in a safe place with your brother. Stay there. I'll work things out for myself."

"Have you called Charlotte?"

"Not yet."

"Well, call her. She'll send you money."

"I will. I want to spend some time alone, thinking about my life. I might try to get some work for a while. I'm not Blanche DuBois in *A Streetcar Named Desire*—I don't want to depend on the kindness of strangers anymore. I'll be all right. Then I'll come back and we'll figure out what to do."

It was then that I told her about the Senetsky school and what had happened. She was very happy for me.

"Oh, you should do it, Rose. Do it."

"I don't know yet," I said. "There's money involved."

"We'll find a way. Do it," she pleaded.

"Mommy, I can't do anything until I know you'll be all right."

"I'll be all right if you will," she promised, "and you will if you have something to achieve. I'll call you in a day or so. I promise. I've been such a selfish, self-absorbed fool and neglected you, Rose. I'm so sorry."

"Mommy..."

"Get yourself in that school. Do it," she said before hanging up.

Evan knew how much I was waiting for her call. He was in the hallway, watching for me. We went into his room and I told him what had happened. He looked very suspicious.

"She's telling me the truth, Evan. Why are your eyes so full of doubt?"

"Remember 'something is rotten in the state of Denmark'?" he said cryptically.

"Yes."

I had no idea what he meant.

"There's something you should know," he said. "I never told you because I didn't want you feeling worse or angrier at your...our father. The night my mother was killed by that drunken driver, she was going to rendczvous with our father. My aunt Charlotte made her go. I overheard their conversation. She wanted her to blackmail him, make his life miserable. I don't think she was going to do that, but I know my aunt Charlotte. When my mother was killed, she felt cheated."

"What does this have to do with what happened to my mother?" I asked.

"Maybe nothing," he said. "I don't know."

He thought a moment and then he said, "Just follow me."

He wheeled out and I followed him to the office. He went to the desk and opened a drawer to take out a checkbook.

"What are you doing?" I asked. He didn't reply. He turned the pages and then he looked up.

"Just as I suspected," he said. "I guess I always had it in the back of my mind, but your mother and Grover seemed so happy together, I didn't want to even suggest such a thing and make you worry more."

"What are you talking about, Evan?"

I came up beside him and he pointed to the record of checks paid. Charlotte had been giving Grover Fleming money.

"I sort of knew that he was one of those Southern gentlemen with a rich name and no bank account," Evan said. "There was a time when he tried to court my mother, but Aunt Charlotte discouraged it. I never liked him much."

"I wish you had told me," I said.

He nodded.

"I wish I had, too."

"Well," we heard, and looked up to see Charlotte in the doorway. "And what do we have here?"

Evan closed the checkbook and backed away from the desk.

"Why did you do this?" I asked.

"Do what?" She entered the office, with a big, sweet, innocent smile on her face.

"Be the devil and tempt my mother into the abyss of self-indulgence," I said.

"My, my, such dramatic words. Evan, you didn't give them to her, did you?"

"She does pretty well for herself, Aunt Charlotte," he said.

"Yes, I suppose she does."

"Why? Why did you arrange for Grover to hurt her like this? Why did you really bring us here?"

Anger deepened the lines in her face and turned her eyes into orbs of darkness and hate.

"Your father destroyed my sister's life. Everything that's happening now is just."

"You're a sick, evil woman," I charged.

"Really? I'm sick and evil?" She smiled and moved closer. "Did I bring this poor child into the world without a father, a child who needs more attention and love than most children? Did I try to buy off my guilt with an occasional check in the mail and keep a poor, innocent girl strung along on promise after promise, lie after lie?"

"But why punish them, Aunt Charlotte?" Evan asked for me.

"She knows. I told her when I first met her," Charlotte said. "The sins of the father are visited on the head of the child."

"You didn't get to punish him, so you decided to punish them?"

"Justice for you and your mother," she told him.

"You never really knew my mother, knew your own sister. She would hate you for what you've done, hate you almost as much as I do now!" he said.

Her cruel smile of victory turned into a sneer.

"Your mother was always too weak and too trusting. That's why she suffered. There are only two kinds of people in the world, Evan, the strong and the weak. I chose to be the strong. Sometimes, the choice is already made for you," she added, looking down at him. "You should be grateful you have me to protect you."

"Like a rabbit's grateful to a snake."

She laughed again.

Then she looked at me sternly.

"I won't blame you if you decide to leave and join your mother wherever she is."

"She's not leaving to join her mother. She's going to a prominent school for the performing arts," Evan said firmly.

"Whatever," Charlotte replied. "I have a dinner date

with Grover. I must get myself ready," she said, then turned and left us.

"She's right," I said, my eyes burning with tears of self-pity and tears of anger. "There are only two kinds of people."

"So you be one of the strong. Succeed. Succeed for both of us, Rose."

"How can I do it, Evan? I don't have the money."

"Yes, you do," he said. "I'm going to give it to you and she can't do anything about it."

I started to shake my head.

"You're my hope, too, now," he said. "Help me get out of this chair, out of this...prison, by being a successful dancer. I'll be there with you whenever I can," he promised.

He reached up for me and I knelt down and hugged him. We held onto each other, tied by blood, tied by dreams, tied by hope and love.

He was able to give me the money. He had funds Aunt Charlotte didn't even know about. He had taken some of his trust fund and played the stock market over the Internet, and he had easy access to the money. The very next day Miss Anderson was able to tell Edmond I would attend his mother's school.

A week later, Mommy called to tell me she had landed a decent job in Atlanta. She was going to work for a local television station. When she had learned what Charlotte had done, she would have nothing more to do with her. She came to my high school graduation and she, Evan, Barry, and I went out to celebrate. Afterward, before she left to return to Atlanta, we had some time together. We sat and had coffee on the patio of a little café.

"I really don't have anyone but myself to blame for what Charlotte did," she told me. "I let myself believe in fairy tales."

"You were very vulnerable, Mommy, and she took advantage of that."

"There's a sign on the wall in the offices where I'm working now. It reads, IF YOU ACT LIKE SHEEP, THEY'LL ACT LIKE WOLVES. Your Daddy used to say that. The trouble is," she added with a thin, little laugh, "we women need to be sheep sometimes. We need to be devoured by a good wolf once in a while."

"Never, Mommy. We never need that."

She shrugged.

"I've never been strong. But you're different, Rose. I'm not worried for you. You're going to make something of yourself. I'm so proud of you."

"I'm worried about you, Mommy."

"Don't," she ordered. "I'll be fine. There's got to be a real prince out there for me somewhere. Someone has the glass slipper that will fit my foot and magically turn me into a princess."

Who's better off? I wondered. People who have no fantasies, no dreams, or those who can't seem to shake them off, who walk about with a hopeful smile and eagerly turn themselves to the sound of any soft voice, any jeweled promise?

We said good-bye and hugged and held each other and promised to stay in very close touch, even when I lived and studied dance in New York. When she walked away, I couldn't help feeling she was the daughter now. I was the mature one. It filled my heart with such fear for her.

Actually, it was harder saying good-bye to Evan. He and Barry were the only people I cared about besides Mommy. I knew I would be able to see Barry in New York since he was attending NYU, but once I left, I had no idea when I would see Evan again. Travel was not going to be easy for him.

On a beautiful afternoon with clouds so white they looked made out of milk, Evan and I said good-bye by his tree.

"Will you be all right here, Evan, living with her still?"

"It doesn't matter. It hasn't up until now. She has her life and I have mine. We have little to do with each other really."

"I don't like the thought that you'll be locked up in your computer world again, never getting out."

"Oh, I'm going to get out more. Don't worry about that. And I'm hoping you'll be on a computer, too, and we can e-mail each other and stuff. We'll talk on the phone and, when you're ready, I'll even come to New York. Don't worry about me now, Rose. Your coming here was the best thing that ever happened to me. Aunt Charlotte doesn't understand. She thinks she got some sort of revenge, but she did me a great favor."

"Me too," I said quickly.

"She's not strong. She's trapped in her own arrogance and conceit. One day she'll wake up and look at herself in the mirror and see only a sour old lady. She'll spend her days in her private hell, believe me."

"You're so wise for someone your age, Evan. I wish I was as wise as you."

"I've had a lot of time to think, study, meditate, I guess. It's made me twice my age, probably. I'm not happy about it. I wish I'd had a normal childhood, too.

"I wish I was out here again, a little boy, holding my mother's hand," he continued, "listening to her read me fairy tales, playing games like deciding what this cloud looks like or that. Pretending instead of analyzing, imagining instead of thinking. You gave me some of that back, Rose."

"Whatever I gave you was only half of what you gave me."

"That figures. I'm your half-brother," he said, joking.

"You're my whole brother. You'll always be," I said with firmness. I kissed him. "You want to come out front to say good-bye for now? Mommy will be here any moment to get me," I said.

He shook his head.

"No. Just walk off, Rose. I'll stay here a while. I've got things to say to the birds, the trees, the clouds. I just want to feel the sun on my face."

I smiled, pressed his hand one more time, and walked away.

I looked back once.

He was sitting upright, looking out at the trees in the distance and holding his head as if his mother was with him, pressing hers to his, and beginning a wonderful new fairy tale.

I could almost hear her voice.

"Once upon a time..."

During the spring of my seventeenth year, I learned a shocking truth about my family.

Neither my mother nor my father wanted me to ever know that there were such dark secrets buried in our family vaults, secrets that deserved to be buried forever.

Daddy once said, "As soon as we're born, we're given private burdens to carry, burdens we simply inherit. Sometimes those are the burdens no one but you can carry for yourself, no matter how much someone loves you and cherishes you, Honey.

"In fact, the truth is, the more you love someone, the more you want to keep him or her from ever knowing the deepest, darkest secrets in your heart."

"Why, Daddy?" I asked.

He smiled.

"We all want to be perfect for the one we love."

That meant no stains, no dark evil, nothing that would bring shame and disgrace along with my name. I knew that.

I also would soon know why it was impossible.

In the spring of my senior year in high school, my uncle Peter was killed when his airplane crashed in the field he was crop-dusting. A witness said the engine just choked and died on him. He was only thirty-five years old, and he had been my first pretend boyfriend. He had taken me flying at least a dozen times in his plane. When he performed his aerial acrobatics with me in the passenger seat beside him, I screamed at the top of my lungs. I screamed with a smile on my face, the way most people do when they have just gone over a particularly steep peak of track on the roller coaster at the Castle Rock Fun Park, which was only a few miles east of Columbus. Uncle Peter had taken me there, too.

He was my father's younger brother, but the five years between them seemed like a gap of centuries when it came to comparing their personalities. Daddy was often almost as serious and religious as Grandad Forman. Both were what anyone would call workaholics on our corn farm—actually, Grandad's five-hundred-acre corn farm. Everything still belonged to Grandad, which was something he never let any of us forget, especially my step-uncle Simon, who lived in a makeshift room over the cow barn. Grandad claimed that way Simon would be close to his work. One of his chores every day was milking and caring for the milk cows. He was the son of Grandad's first wife, Tess. Simon had just been born when Tess married Grandad, but Grandad always regarded him as if he were an illegitimate child, working him hard and treating him like he was outside the family or the village idiot.

There were only very rare times when all of us, my uncle Peter, my father and mother, and my step-uncle Simon would be around Grandad's dark oak dining room table, reciting grace and enjoying a meal and an evening together. However, when we were, it was easy to scc the vast differences among everyone.

Simon was the biggest of the men in our family. His father had been a very big man, six foot five and nearly three hundred pounds. Simon had grown very quickly—too quickly, according to Grandad Forman, who claimed Uncle Simon's body drained too much from his brain in the process. Always taller than anyone his age, Simon was large, towering, and lanky, awkward for almost anything but heavy manual labor, which only made him more massive and stronger.

Simon never did well in school. Grandad claimed the teachers told him Simon was barely a shade or two above mentally retarded. I never believed that to be true. I knew in my heart he simply would rather be outside and couldn't keep his eyes from the classroom windows, mesmerized by the flight of a bird or even the mad circling of insects.

Anyone would look small beside Simon, but Uncle Peter was barely five foot nine and slim. He had as big an appetite as my daddy or even as Simon at times, but he was always moving, joking, singing or dancing. He had long, flaxen hair, green eyes, and a smile that could beam good feelings across our biggest cornfield.

Sometimes for fun at dinner—when Uncle Simon was permitted to eat with us—Uncle Peter would challenge him to an arm wrestle and put his graceful, almost feminine fingers into the cavern of Uncle Simon's bear-claw palm. Uncle Simon would smile at Uncle Peter's great effort to move his arm back a tenth of an inch. Once, he even put both his hands in one of Uncle Simon's and then he got up and threw his whole body into the effort, while Uncle Simon sat there as unmoving as a giant boulder. Grandad Forman called him an idiot and ordered them both to stop their tomfoolery at his dinner table, but not as gruffly as he ordered me or Daddy or even Mommy when he wanted us to perform some chore or obey some command.

I always felt Grandad Forman was less severe on Uncle Peter. If Grandad had any kind bones in his body, he turned them only on him, favoring him as much or as best he could favor anyone. From the pictures I saw of her, Uncle Peter did look more like his mother than he did Grandad, and I wondered if that was what Grandad saw in him whenever he looked at him. His and Daddy's mother was Tess's sister, Jennie, whom Grandad married a year after Tess's death from breast cancer. Simon was only three and needed a mother, but after a little more than eight years of marriage, Grandad lost Jennie, too.

According to everything I've ever heard about her, my grandma Jennie was a sweet, kind and loving woman who treated Uncle Simon well, too well for Grandad's liking. It wasn't until after she had died of a heart attack that he moved Simon out of the house and into the barn. According to Uncle Peter, and even Daddy, she wouldn't have tolerated it, even though she was too meek and servile in every other way and permitted Grandad to work her to death. She was often seen beside him in the fields, despite a full day of house cleaning and cooking.

However, Grandad Forman had a religious philosophy that prevented him from ever taking responsibility for anything that had happened to his family or anyone else with whom he might have come into contact. He believed bad things happened to people as a result of their own evil thoughts, evil deeds. God, he preached, punishes us on earth and rewards us on earth. If something terrible happens to someone we all thought was a good person, we must understand that we didn't know what was in his or her heart and in his or her past. God sees all. Grandad was so vehement about this that he often made me feel God was spying on me every moment of the day, and if I should stray so much as an iota from the Good Book or the Commandments, I would be struck down with the speed of a bolt of lightning.

Consequently, Grandad Forman did not cry at funerals, and when the horrible news about Uncle Peter was brought to our house, he absorbed and accepted it, lowered his head, and went out to work in the field just as he had planned.

Mommy was nearly inconsolable. I believe she loved Uncle Peter almost as much as she loved Daddy, almost as much as I loved him. We cried and held each other. Daddy went off to mourn privately, I know. Uncle Simon raged like a wild beast in his barn. We could hear the metal tools being flung against the walls, and then he marched out and took hold of a good size sapling he had planted seven years before and put all of his sorrow into a gigantic effort to lift it out of the earth, roots and all, which he did.

"Lunatic," Grandad said when he saw what he had done. "God will punish him for that."

That evening I sat on the porch steps and stared up at the stars. I had no appetite at dinner and couldn't pronounce a syllable of grace. I wasn't in the mood to thank God for anything, least of all food, but Grandad thought wasting food was one of the worst sins anyone could commit, so I forced myself to swallow, practically without chewing. Mommy, who cooked and cleaned and kept house for him as well as for Daddy and me, choked back her tears, but sniffled too often for Grandad's liking. He chastised her: "It's God's will, and His will be done. So stop your confounded sobbing at dinner."

I looked to Daddy to see if he would speak up in her defense, but he stared forward, muted by his sorrow. Unlike Uncle Peter, Daddy never stood up to Grandad. He was a quiet man, strong and compassionate in his own way, but always, it seemed to me, caught in Grandad's shadow. As I grew older, I became more and more curious about Daddy's relationship with Grandad Forman. I sensed there was something beyond the biblical commandment to honor your parents. There was something else between them, some deep family secret that kept Daddy's eyes from ever turning furious and intent on Grandad, no matter what he said or did to him or to Mommy and me. Rarely did either he or Grandad raise their voices against each other. Grandad's voice was raised in his glaring eyes rather than his clicking tongue, and Daddy choked back any resistance, disapproval, or complaint.

He seemed to go at his work with a fury built out of a need to channel all his unhappiness into something that would please Grandad and at the same time give himself some respite, some form of release from the tension that loomed continuously over us all.

Grandad Forman was still a powerful man, even in his early seventies. He was about six foot three himself, but walked with stooped shoulders. He reminded me of a closed fist: tight, powerful, even lethal.

"Life's got to go on," he declared, lecturing to Mommy. "It's God's gift, and we don't turn our backs on it."

Almost for spite, to show us he practiced what he preached, he ate with just as much vigor and appetite as he had ever done and looked to us to do the same.

I was glad when I could get away from him.

On my tenth birthday, Uncle Peter had bought me a violin. It was very expensive, and Grandad Forman complained for days about the "waste of so much money." But I had taken some lessons at school and talked about how I had enjoyed playing a violin.

"That's what we need around here," Uncle Peter had decided, "some good music. Honey's just the one to make it for us."

He even paid for my private lessons. My teacher, Clarence Wengrow, claimed I had a natural inclination for it and early on recommended I think seriously about attending a school of performing arts somewhere. Grandad Forman thought that was pure nonsense and would actually become angry if we discussed anything about my music at dinner, slapping the table so hard he would make the dishes dance. Uncle Peter tried to get him to appreciate music, but Grandad had a strict puritanical view of it as another vehicle upon which the devil rode into our hearts and souls. It took us away from hard work and prayer, and that was always dangerous.

Grandad could go on and on like a hell-and-damnation preacher. Daddy would sit with his head bowed, his eyes closed, like someone just trying to wait out some pain. Most of the time Mommy ignored Grandad, but Uncle Peter always wore a soft smile, as if he found his father quaint, amusing.

I couldn't get Uncle Peter's smile out of my eyes that first night of his death. I heard his laughter and heard him call my name. He loved teasing me about it. Uncle Peter would sing, "We've got Honey. We've got sugar, but Honey is the sweet one for me."

He would laugh and throw his arm around my shoulders and kiss the top of my hair, pretending he had just swallowed the most delicious tablespoon of honey in the world.

How could someone with so much life and love in him be snuffed out like a candle in seconds? I wondered. Why would God let this happen? Could Grandad Forman be right? It made no sense to me. I wouldn't accept it. I would never permit myself to think the smallest bad thing about Uncle Peter. He had no secret evil, in his heart or otherwise. It was all simply a galactic mistake, a gross error. God had made a wrong decision or failed to catch it in time. However, I knew if I so much as suggested such a thing in front of Grandad, he would fly into a hurricane of rage.

"Oh, dear God," I prayed, "surely You can right the wrong, correct the error. Turn us back a day and make this day disappear forever," I begged.

Then I picked up my violin and played, my music flowing out into the night.

Grandad would wave his hand as if he was chasing away gnats and walk off, his head down, his long arms swinging in rhythm to his plodding gait.

When did he ever laugh? When did he ever feel happy or good about himself? Why was he so worried about sinning and going to hell?

Maybe he thought he was already in hell. It wasn't to be very long before I would understand why.

Turn the page for a preview of
FLOWERS IN THE ATTIC. . . .

The train lumbered through a dark and starry night, heading toward a distant mountain estate in Virginia. We passed many a sleepy town and village, and scattered farmhouses where golden rectangles of light were the only evidence to show they were there at all. My brother and I didn't want to fall asleep and miss out on anything, and oh, did we have a lot to talk about! Mostly we speculated on that grand, rich house where we would live in splendor, and eat from golden plates, and be served by a butler wearing livery. And I supposed I'd have my own maid to lay out my clothes, draw my bath, brush my hair, and jump when I commanded.

While my brother and I speculated on how we would spend our money, the portly, balding conductor entered our small compartment and gazed admiringly at our mother before he softly spoke: "Mrs. Patterson, in fifteen minutes we'll reach your depot."

Now why was he calling her "Mrs. Patterson"? I wondered. I shot a questioning look at Christopher, who also seemed perplexed by this.

Jolted awake, appearing startled and disoriented, Momma's eyes flew wide open. Her gaze jumped from the conductor, who hovered so close above her, over to Christopher and me, and then she looked down in despair at the sleeping twins. "Yes, thank you," she said to the conductor, who was still watching her with great approval and admiration. "Don't fear, we'll be ready to leave."

"Ma'am," he said, most concerned when he glanced at his pocket watch, "it's three o'clock in the morning. Will someone be there to meet you?"

"It's all right," assured our mother.

"Ma'am, it's very dark out there."

"I could find my way home asleep."

The grandfatherly conductor wasn't satisfied with this. "Lady," he said, "we are letting you and your children off in the middle of nowhere. There's not a house in sight."

To forbid any further questioning, Momma answered in her most arrogant manner, "Someone *is* meeting us." Funny how she could put on that kind of haughty manner like a hat.

It was totally dark when we stepped from the train, and as the conductor had warned, there was not a house in sight. Alone in the night, far from any sign of civilization, we stood and waved good-bye to the conductor on the train steps, holding on by one hand, waving with the other. His expression revealed that he wasn't too happy about leaving "Mrs. Patterson" and her brood of four sleepy children waiting for someone coming in a car. I looked around and saw nothing but a rusty, tin roof supported by four wooden posts, and a rickety green bench.

We were surrounded by fields and meadows. From the deep woods in back of the "depot," something made a weird noise. I jumped and spun about to see what it was, making Christopher laugh. "That was only an owl! Did you think it was a ghost?"

"Now there is to be none of that!" said Momma sharply. "We have to hurry. It's a long, long walk to my home, and we have to reach there before dawn, when the servants get up."

How strange. "Why?" I asked. "And why did that conductor call you Mrs. Patterson?"

"Cathy, I don't have time to explain to you now. We've got to walk fast." She bent to pick up the two heaviest suitcases. Christopher and I were forced to carry the twins, who were too sleepy to walk.

"Momma!" I cried out, when we had moved on a few steps, "the conductor forgot to give us *your* two suitcases!"

"It's all right, Cathy," she said breathlessly, as if the two suitcases she was carrying were enough to tax her strength. "I asked the conductor to take my two bags on to Charlottesville and put them in a locker for me to pick up tomorrow morning."

"Why would you do that?" asked Christopher.

"Well, for one thing, I certainly couldn't handle *four* suitcases, could I? And, for another thing, I want the chance to talk to my father first before he learns about you. And it just wouldn't seem right if I arrived home in the middle of the night after being gone for fifteen years, now would it?"

It sounded reasonable, I guess, for we did have all we could handle. We set off, tagging along behind our mother, over uneven ground, following faint paths between rocks and trees and shrubbery that clawed at our clothes. We trekked a long, long way. Christopher and I became tired, irritable, as the twins grew heavier, and our arms began to ache. We complained, we nagged, we dragged our feet, wanting to sit down and rest. We wanted to be back in our own beds, with our own things—better than here—better than that big old house with servants and grandparents we didn't even know.

"Wake up the twins!" snapped Momma, grown impatient with our complaining. "Stand them on their feet, and force them to walk." Then she mumbled something faint into the collar of her jacket that just barely reached my ears: "Lord knows, they'd better walk outside while they can."

A ripple of apprehension shot down my spine. I glanced at my older brother to see if he'd heard, just as he turned his head to look at me. He smiled. I smiled in return.

Tomorrow, when Momma arrived at a proper time, in a taxi, she would go to the sick grandfather and she'd smile, and she'd speak, and he'd be charmed, won over. Just one look at her lovely face, and just one word from her soft beautiful voice, and he'd hold out his arms, and forgive her for whatever she'd done to make her "fall from grace."

From what she'd already told us, her father was a cantankerous *old* man, for sixty-six did seem like incredibly old age to me. And a man on the verge of death couldn't afford to hold grudges against his sole remaining child, a daughter he'd once loved very much. Then she'd bring us down from the bedroom, and we'd be looking our best, and acting our sweetest selves, and he'd soon see we weren't ugly, or really bad, and nobody, absolutely nobody with a heart could resist loving the twins. And just wait until Grandfather learned how smart Christopher was!

The air was cool and sharply pungent. Though Momma called this hill country, those shadowy, high forms in the distance looked like mountains to me. I stared up at the sky. Why did it seem to be looking down at me with pity, making me feel ant-sized, overwhelmed, completely insignificant? It was too big, that sky, too beautiful, and it filled me with a strange sense of foreboding.

We came at last upon a cluster of large and very fine homes, nestled on a steep hillside. Stealthily, we approached the largest and, by far, the grandest of all the sleeping mountain homes.

We circled that enormous house, almost on tiptoes. At the back door, an old lady let us in. She must have been waiting, and seen us coming, for she opened that door so readily we didn't even have to knock. Just like thieves in the night, we stole silently inside. Not a word did she speak to welcome us. Could this be one of the servants? I wondered.

Immediately we were inside the dark house, and she hustled us up a steep and narrow back staircase, not allowing us one second to pause and take a look around the grand rooms we only glimpsed in our swift passage. She led us down many halls, past many closed doors, and finally we came to an end room, where she swung open a door and gestured us inside. It was a relief to have our long night journey over, and be in a large bedroom where a single lamp was lit. The old woman turned to look us over as she closed the heavy door to the hall and leaned against it.

She spoke, and I was jolted. "Just as you said, Corrine. Your children are beautiful."

There she was, paying us a compliment that should warm our hearts—but it chilled mine. Her voice was cold and uncaring, as if we were without ears to hear, and without minds to comprehend her displeasure, despite her flattery.

"But are you sure they are intelligent? Do they have some invisible afflictions not apparent to the eyes?"

"None!" cried our mother, taking offense, as did I. "My children are perfect, as you can plainly see, physically and mentally!" She glared at that old woman in gray before she squatted down on her heels and began to undress Carrie, who was nodding on her feet. I knelt before Cory and unbuttoned his small blue jacket, as Christopher lifted one of the suitcases up on one of the big beds. He opened it and took out two pairs of small yellow pajamas with feet.

Furtively, as I helped Cory off with his clothes and into his yellow pajamas, I studied that tall, big woman, who was, I presumed, our grandmother.

Her nose was an eagle's beak, her shoulders were wide, and her mouth was like a thin, crooked knife slash. Her dress, of gray taffeta, had a diamond brooch at the throat of a high, severe neckline. Nothing about her appeared soft or yielding; even her bosom looked like twin hills of concrete. There would be no funning with her, as we had played with our mother and father.

I didn't like her. I wanted to go home. My lips quivered.

How could such a woman as this make someone as lovely and sweet as our mother? From whom had our mother inherited her beauty, her gaiety? I shivered, and tried to forbid those tears that welled in my eyes. Momma had prepared us in advance for an unloving, uncaring, unrelenting grandfather—but the grandmother who had arranged for our coming—she came as a harsh, astonishing surprise. I blinked back my tears. But to reassure me, there was our mother smiling warmly as she lifted a pajamaed Cory into one of the big beds, and then she put Carrie in beside him. Oh, how they did look sweet, lying there, like big, rosy-cheeked dolls. Momma leaned over the twins and pressed kisses on their flushed cheeks, and her hand tenderly brushed back the curls on their foreheads. "Good night, my darlings," she whispered in the loving voice we knew so well.

The twins didn't hear. Already they were deeply asleep.

However, standing firmly as a rooted tree, the grandmother was obviously displeased as she gazed upon the twins in one bed, then over to where Christopher and I were huddled close together. We were tired, and half-supporting each other. Strong disapproval glinted in her gray-stone eyes; Momma seemed to understand, although I did not. Momma's face flushed as the grandmother said, "Your two older children cannot sleep in one bed!"

"They're only children," Momma flared back with unusual fire. "You have a nasty, suspicious mind! Christopher and Cathy are innocent!"

"Innocent?" she snapped back, her mean look so sharp it could cut and draw blood. "That is exactly what your father and I always presumed about you and your half-uncle!"

"If you think like that, then give them separate rooms and separate beds."

"That is impossible," the grandmother said. "This is the only bedroom with its own adjoining bath, and where my husband won't hear them walking overhead, or flushing the toilet. If they are separated, and scattered about all over upstairs, he will hear their voices, or their noise, or the servants will. This is the only safe room."

Safe room? We were going to sleep, all of us, in only one room? In a grand, rich house with twenty, thirty, forty rooms, we were going to stay in one room? Even so, now that I gave it more thought, I didn't want to be in a room alone in this mammoth house.

"Put the two girls in one bed, and the two boys in the other," the grandmother ordered.

Momma lifted Cory and put him in the remaining double bed, thus, casually establishing the way it was to be from then on.

The old woman turned her hard gaze on me, then on Christopher. "Now hear this," she began like a drill sergeant, "it will be up to you two older children to keep the younger ones quiet. Keep this always in your minds: if your grandfather learns you are up here, then he will throw all of you out without one red penny—*after* he has severely punished you for being alive! You will not yell, or cry, or run about to pound on the ceilings below. When your mother and I leave this room tonight, I will close and lock the door behind me. Until the day your grandfather dies, you are here, but you don't really exist."

Oh, God! This couldn't be true! She was lying, wasn't she? Saying mean things just to scare us. I tried to look at Momma, but she had turned her back and her head was lowered, but her shoulders sagged and quivered as if she were crying.

Panic filled me....